## *More Praise for Elwin*
## The Jack Daniels Se

"Cotman has an amazing voice, and his fabulist descriptions are so vividly communicated, they almost lift from the page and become three-dimensional beings that are impossible images to forget."

—Savannah Schroll Guz, author of *American Soma*

"Mr. Cotman's interests are wide-ranging: Punk rock intersects with D.C.'s Dominican community, African American folktale intersects with Greek myth, Goth teen suburban angst in 1990s Ohio sits side by side with racist atrocity in the pre-Civil Rights South, and magic is going on. Yeah, there's magic in some of these stories, but the real magic is in Cotman's words themselves—stark and deadpan one moment, lushly descriptive the next."

—Michael S. Begnal, author of *Ancestor Worship*

"Cotman's breadth and depth of characterization amaze, as you are swept by his words into lives that are as familiar as next door and into situations as fantastic as Narnia or Neverland. Funny, fresh and thought-provoking on all levels, Cotman's voice soon will take a place with past masters like Octavia Butler, Michael Moorcock and Jonathan Maberry on the fantasy scene."

—*Critic Studio*

"This is not always a comfortable book to read, but it is a magnificent one. *The Jack Daniels Sessions EP* is comprised of short stories and vignettes that flow into one another like the Mississippi rushes over the Delta. Elwin Cotman is a writer, an activist, a performance artist and above all, an impeccable storyteller."

—*Cabinet de Fées*

# The Jack Daniels Sessions EP

Elwin Cotman

To Amy & Daniel, All the best!

Elwin M Cotman

THE JACK DANIELS SESSIONS EP



Cover by Daniel McCloskey

Illustrations by Rachel Dorrett

Published by Six Gallery Press

ISBN: 978-1-926616-17-9

"When the Law Come" first published in *The Dirty Napkin*, Fall 2009

Third Printing, November 2012

Tracks

1. Safe Space
2. When the Law Come
3. Dead Teenagers
4. How Brother Roy Lost His Dog, Twice
5. Assistant

# SAFE SPACE

*"You are young...but we are old. The world was wild with youth when we were reared. You and your tribe shall pass, but we are invincible, indestructible."*
—Robert E. Howard
"The Shadow Kingdom"

*All-Ages Eve of War Punkstravaganza!*

**Third Term Abortion**
Legendary D.C. hardcore, reunited for the 1st time since 1985
**Molly Ringworm**
Homegrown DIY Anarcho-Punk
**The Yes-Men**
Hardcore antics from Baltimore

$7 admission!!!
At the 9:30 Club!!!
9:30 pm
Jan. 15, in the Year of Our War Nineteen Ninety-One!!!

Lips and dark skin.

That was how Mack Ramirez recognized Ingrid Garcia, as he sat smoking weed on his mom's porch and saw what looked like a bag lady pushing a brand-new Schwinn bicycle down the sidewalk. Ingrid grew up with him in the Adams Morgan area of DC, before he left for college in Ohio, and she figured in many of his memories: running around his apartment naked while his mom babysat her, playing hooky downtown with their friends, looking dazzling at senior prom. Back then he viewed her, like all beautiful girls, in parts. Thick legs, full hips, sleek black hair, juicy lips and dark skin. Dark coffee skin, tar baby skin, skin so black it looked burnt.

Ingrid was a typical Dominican girl. Headstrong, quick to anger, loyal to her family, fierce in her friendship. While all the other girls listened to Michael Jackson and New Edition, she spun the Clash on her record player and stuck New York Dolls pins on her Lincoln High School blazer.

Punk rock had consumed her since the last time he saw her. Instead of the girl he knew, he saw a scarecrow, tattooed and lean as a strip of gristle. Black skirt, flannel shirt around her waist, steel-toe boots, a black sweatshirt with a big patch on the back that said BAD BRAINS. Sharp angles replaced her curves, the swell of breast under her shirt the only clear sign of her femininity.

Mack called out to her, and she ran to him with a smile. He hugged her in his big arms. She was bald, save for a single lock of peroxide-blond hair falling over her right eye. Mack noticed the stares of his friends on the porch, felt embarrassed holding this dirty person. He kept their conversation short. Ingrid invited him to see her band, Molly Ringworm, at the 9:30 Club. "We're not too good right now," she admitted sheepishly, her breath frosting in the winter air. "But even if we suck, it'll still be entertaining." Smiling sweetly, she walked off with her bike.

The smell hit him the moment he entered. A lethal combination of nicotine, urine, vomit and sweat, combined with the suffocating tobacco smoke that fogged the club. Raucous music blasted from the stage, a band called The Yes-Men torturing their instruments. Mack's friends followed him. Rough and ready Dominicans he'd grown up with, they wore tight jeans, neon-colored shirts, leather jackets and fedoras. They trailed Mack to the floor, looking around disgustedly. Mack wore a goosedown coat, green- and white-checkered vest, neon green parachute pants and an Africa-shaped pendant on a gold chain. He was a big man; you could seat two full-grown people on his shoulders. He shook out his stiff limbs, brushed the snowflakes off his flat-top fade haircut. Warmth returned to his body, an almost painful sensation. Mack peered over the sardine-packed mass of mohawks, looking for Ingrid. The only person who intrigued him enough to make him spend his last night in DC at a punk club that smelled like rat piss.

“Why are we here, man?” asked one of his friends, who also wore a flat-top.

“Just to see Ingrid,” Mack promised. “Then we out.” A boy with a rainbow-colored mohawk hurried past them. “Look at that motherfucker! Looking like a Skittle-head rooster!”

Even Mack had heard of the DC hardcore legends Third Term Abortion. He could see them tuning their instruments by the stage. They looked more like he expected fans of Third Term to look than the actual band: fat, balding men in too-small leather jackets, cradling 40 ounces and tilting on their feet like weather vanes.

Mack smiled at the irony of this white “music” club squatting so close to Adams Morgan, a traditionally immigrant neighborhood. His part of town had always bounced to the rhythm of Samba; the smell of tortilla, *injera* and lasagna flavored the air. Still, he saw the McDonalds and Taco Bells encroaching from other neighborhoods, slowly robbing DC of its culture. Mack knew all about the city’s history. Before DC’s black renaissance became a paragraph at the tail-end of a textbook, it was something people lived and sang and smelled and felt. Mack heard the stories from older residents who didn’t even realize what they had until they lost it. An emptiness in them where used to be grandeur. An absence of pride.

Mack and his friends pushed through the punks like a neon barge through a black sea. All the kids wore the punk uniform: mohawks, patches on their hand-me-down pants, Crass and Government Issue and Minor Threat pins on their black sweaters. Only a few stood out, and the sight of them prickled Mack’s skin.

Looking like Mad Max villains in their spike-studded leather, three skinheads stood in the back of the club, by the bulletin board riddled with staples and thumb tacks. One was a mountainous man blocking the exit door like a brick wall. Another was a bald woman with a wide, sagging paunch like a slovenly man’s, her face pinched like she smelled something sour. The third, a leathery man, smoked a cigarette and blew it out his nostrils. Tall and angular, with a look on his face like Snoopy in the *Peanuts* comics; completely aloof, so condescending he couldn’t bother opening his eyes to look at the people around him.

In the dim light, the air around them seemed to shimmer like on a hot day. Probably because of the smoke, Mack figured. He squinted, took a closer look. Without opening his eyes, the tall one turned his head toward him, an unreadable expression on his ruddy face. A feeling of unreality came over Mack; the very air felt tense and charged. No longer feeling like the baddest dude in the club, he still managed to keep his head high as his group passed them.

Onstage, a shirtless man with a mohawk screamed his throat to shreds. "Oh," Mack said, watching the scene in front of the stage with interest. "What is this?" Punks swinging their arms, shoving each other, cartwheeling and spin-kicking. A grimy, sweaty, bone-crunching dance of aggression. One man piggy-backed on another, grabbed the ceiling pipework and hung from it. Another man launched himself from one side of the pit to the next, bouncing off onlookers. Watching this chaos, a grin crept across Mack's face.

"A mosh pit? Now *that's* what I'm talkin' 'bout!" With a roar, he and his friends charged like bulls into the pit. Shoulder tackling and shoving, knocking punk kids on the floor. In a minute, only they remained. "Hey," Mack laughed, looking around, "where'd everybody go?"

Suddenly, someone dashed past him, climbed onstage. Ingrid, wearing a black tank top. She leaned on the lead singer, the two of them screaming in the mic:

Freedom! I'll fuck you for it!
Freedom! I'll suck your dick!
Please, sir, please, sir, pretty please, sir
I'll get right down on my knees, sir
Listen to me, don't ignore it
Human rights! I'll fuck you for it!

Seeing Mack, she stage-dove into his arms. An unwashed bohemian stench wafted from her armpit afros. Laughing, Mack gave her a piggyback ride around the pit. She headbanged on top of him, her one lock whipping about her face.

They ran to the back of the club. Mack embraced her, crushing her little body against his. "You had fun, huh?" she said, the sweaty lock plastered to her forehead.

Mack barked a laugh. "Man, them white dudes gonna go home like, 'Duuuude, there were these black guys at the show, duuuude. They were too rough, duuuude. I'll be sore for a week, duuuude.'"

Ingrid led him to a table covered in bags of bagels, a soggy box of apples, a pan of green pepper omelet. Spread on the table were small black-and-white 'zines with names like "Kill your TV," "Fuck Radio" and "Annie Oakley's Gun." Reaching for an apple, Mack lightly bumped a white punk's arm. "My fault, homey," he said.

The punk backed up, obviously nervous. Laughing at him, Mack picked up the apple, wiped it on his shirt, tossed it in the air, missed. It rolled across the floor.

"You dropped it!" Ingrid screamed in his ear. "Trying to act tough and you drop the damn thing! Smooth, man. Smooth."

"Shut up," Mack chuckled. "I should be careful about scaring these white people, though. Somebody might call the police up in here." He inspected a rock-hard bagel, cautiously. "This looks like you got it out the trash."

"We did." Ingrid bit her lip. "Well, the stuff we didn't steal."

*Cargo pants were the trick. Lots of pockets, so the store clerks don't see you slip in a spool of twine or sparkly fabric, buttons or a tube of glitter paint. Ingrid prowled the craft store, picking up whatever caught her eye. Waiting for the employee pushing the shopping cart to pass the aisle, she dropped paintbrushes down her many pockets. Two cans of black and red spraypaint disappeared in her sweater.*

*Ingrid heard a clerk coming and turned abruptly, hitting her chest on a shelf. A loud hissing sound. Looking down, she saw spraypaint spread over her sweater like a bloodstain. Laughing, she folded her arms over her chest and hurried outside.*

"So you a klepto?" Mack asked. They sat on an old pleather couch. Mack's friends took a smoke break outside, and he knew they would leave right after. Every few seconds, a beer bottle clattered on the floor.

Ingrid finished her omelet, belched. Absentmindedly, she strummed her electric guitar: a cherry-red Ibanez with six glowing strings. Ingrid's tattoos blended into her black skin, forcing Mack to look closer. A circle- A on her chest; a star in the hollow of her throat; a raised fist on her right shoulder; a huge Maori tattoo twisting maze-like up her left arm. The words D.C. PUNK in cursive on her right arm like the name of a boyfriend.

"I don't think of it as stealing." It felt strange, hearing Ingrid's carefree voice come out this raggedy creature. "I only steal from businesses, not people. They steal from us. Why can't we steal from them?"

"You only steal from businesses, huh?" Mack smiled sardonically. "That bike yesterday didn't look like it came from no business, you stealer."

"Hey, the kid in that coffee shop was obviously bourgeois. Her folks can buy her a new one. I needed it more than she did. What can I say? I'm an anarchist."

Mack chuckled. He knew anarchists in college: white punks who grew up in the suburbs but intentionally lived like homeless people. At least until they joined their uncles' law firms. "Do you dumpster dive?" he asked playfully. "Do you hitchhike? Do you squat in buildings?"

"Maybe I do all of that."

"Are there any other black punks in this entire town except you? 'Cause I don't see too much diversity around here."

"Plenty. Bad Brains is all black, and they're one of the original DC hardcore bands."

"What convinced you to do this to your hair?" He flipped her blond lock.

Ingrid started groping his flat-top. "What convinced you to get this shit? You wanted to use your head as a table? Can you put plates up there? And don't get me started on them limegreen Ali Baba pants, homey. Looking like a broke-ass MC Hammer."

"A'ight! A'ight!" he said, patting his flat-top back in place. No matter how much she changed, she was still a *Dominicana*. "Don't be cruel."

Now Ingrid laughed. "So, I hear you're moving tomorrow."

"Yeah. How'd you hear?"

"I ran into your mom at the grocery the other day. She looks great. Wouldn't stop talking about how proud she is of you, too. How you've got this great new job." Mack smiled. He was the first person in his family to graduate college. His *madre* wouldn't let him, or anyone else in the neighborhood, forget. "So when're you leaving?"

"Ten in the morning. My brother helped me pack my stuff this afternoon. I'm driving all the way to LA."

"Exciting. What are you doing there?"

"Computer tech stuff for Apple. I mean, it ain't the best in the world…"

"But it'll get you the hell out of DC. I'm real happy for you, Mack."

The Yes-Men waved to Ingrid as they walked by, carrying their instruments to their car. They were congratulating each other on the time they ripped off some skinheads. His stomach knotting, Mack saw the three skinheads exchange glances, then follow the band out the club.

"That's a nice guitar," he said, eying the glistening maplewood.

"Yeah, I stole it." Ingrid plucked a string, put her ear close to the vibrating steel thread. She smiled, as if the guitar was whispering a secret. "So, what have you been up to on your last day?" she asked him.

"You know," he said, "watchin' a little football…"

"Watchin' a little football," she mimicked, "liftin' some weights, drinkin' a little forty, playin' a little Nin-ten-do."

Mack smiled. He'd done all of that.

"Yo, Ingrid!" A dreadlocked white person who could have been man or woman high-fived her. One look at Mack and it continued on its way. Mack gave Ingrid a wry look.

"Oh, stop it," Ingrid said.

"That dude's looking a little *kuntsi*."

"That 'dude' is transgendered." A fire burned in her eyes, one he didn't want to touch. "And her name is Soap."

"He gonna name himself after something he don't use?"

"*She*."

Mack let the matter drop. He had no desire to talk about faggots.

"How are things going with your band?"

"Good." She smiled again. "I mean, we got this gig, right? We *did* get into a fight the other day."

"What? Some white dudes was fucking with you?"

"Chill out. They were white, but the real problem is they were douchebags. We were playing this show, and there were just a bunch of drunk scumfucks there. I'm onstage talking about Iraq and how fucked up it is they're starting a war for Texaco, and some skinhead's like, 'Shut the fuck up!' So I call him out, like, 'That's real clever. Do you have anything to back up why I should shut up?' And he just comes back with stupid insults. Then this guy starts pushing my friends, whips out his dick, says all anarchists are faggots and tells me he's gonna fuck me like I've never been fucked before."

"What happened after that?" Mack asked, absolutely bewildered.

"I hit him in the dick with my mic stand. The whole thing turned into a brawl. I broke some girl's nose, and I stomped on some dude." Ingrid shrugged. "Whatever. I mean, I don't like fighting, but I'm *so sick* of these drunk assholes."

Mack's lip curled. "Man, who are these dudes? These white people wanna mess with my girl? Sheeeeit. Tell me who these people are. I'll make a few calls, roll up in there with a couple Dominicans..."

"It's cool. Some people come to shows just to drink and cause trouble. Fuck that. Punk shows should be a safe space, y'know? That's a big reason why I'm straight edge. No drugs, no alcohol. Beer at shows equals bad news. I'm only playing this show because it's Third Term's reunion. They're great guys, despite the fact they're drunks." Mack saw the lead singer of Third Term Abortion race to the restroom, squeezing his bulk in a tiny stall. "I was pissed off about those fliers, though. 'Eve of War Punkstravaganza.' People are about to die. How could you make fun of that?"

Mack thought of the skinheads, who'd left him with a sense of foreboding as great as their physical presence. He swallowed. "You might want to slow down on this shit," he said. "At least ease up with the stealing."

"Mmm...Nah. Thanks for the concern, though. *Dad*." She hoisted her guitar onto her shoulder. The six strings shone like slivers of spun moonlight. "Well, my band's up. Wish me luck."

"Don't steal nothin' while you up there."

Giving him an affectionate middle finger, Ingrid ran onstage, the guitar slung across her back like a battleaxe ready to be unsheathed.

*She tried on clothes with the glee of a child making a Halloween costume. Khakis, Abercrombie sweater dresses, acid-washed jeans, Keds sneakers. "How do I look?" Ingrid posed for her friends in a Howard University sweatshirt, black spandex pants, fanny pack, a beret covering her bald head. She felt like a girl on* Saved by the Bell. *Her friends assured her that she looked totally hot.*

*Clad in her scamouflage, Ingrid walked into the grocery armed with a tote bag and a receipt she'd picked off the street. She couldn't decide whether to get the regular or vanilla soy milk, so she got both. Powdered donuts, fabric softener, granola, nutmeg, pancake mix, cinnamon and a pound of sugar. Ingrid liked Jiffy better than Planters, but Planters had less fat. She added both jars to the tote bag.*

*"Ingrid!"*

*"Oh!" Ingrid exclaimed. "Hi, Miss Ramirez!"*

*Miss Ramirez was a round, sweet-natured woman with a platinum blond perm that looked like the swirls on a lemon birthday cake. "You look nice," she said, hugging Ingrid in her fat arms. "Not so wild like usual." With typical bluntness, she took off Ingrid's beret and ruffled her lock.*

*"Well, I'm trying out a new style, I guess." Ingrid almost said she'd turned over a new leaf and was going mainstream, but she couldn't hide anything from this woman. All Dominican mothers in the neighborhood knew each other. Miss Ramirez probably had sangria with her mom, listened to her lament about her embarrassing, ne'er-do-well daughter. If so, Miss Ramirez didn't say it, cheerfully going on about her son Mack's achievements. Graduating Oberlin magna cum laude, tutoring at the local youth center, getting hired by Apple. As the conversation went on, Ingrid found herself lying. Saying she was looking into community college, had an interest in teaching, had a job at a coffee shop in Dupont*

*Circle. It came naturally to her, and she felt a little ashamed for it.*

*Ingrid flashed the receipt to the security guard on the way out. He wished her a good night. Wistfully, she strolled down the snow-covered sidewalk, swinging her bag from side to side and breathing the crisp night air.*

Ingrid held the guitar uncertainly, made a few practice strums. Beside her, a teenage-looking guy tuned his bass, and a woman, even more punkish than Ingrid, sat behind the drum kit. A wave of feedback from the amplifier drilled into Mack's ears. "Sorry," said Ingrid. "How're y'all doing?"

The punks hollered back at her. Mack planted himself in the middle of the pit so he could get a good look. He wondered at these new feelings he had. All those years they had been close, and she as beautiful a girl to ever don jeans shorts in the summer, to eat mangoes and gossip at the *taquerias* on Columbia Road. Yet he never thought of her as anything more than his *hermanita*. Oh, there were stirrings here and there. They'd danced together at senior prom, to the throwback jam. What was it? Ah, yes. "Love Me in a Special Way" by DeBarge. Mack had to hunch down, she had to stand on tiptoes; her body pressed against his made his heart beat until it felt overwhelming. The memory gave him a warm feeling, but nothing like the electric tingle in his throat as he watched her tune the strings. She wasn't unattractive; her appearance was strong and dangerous. She was self-sufficient, and who doesn't like that in a woman? So different, yet in a way more of herself, like she had evolved. He liked that. His attraction didn't make complete sense to him, which he also liked.

"Yo, I think she got a back-up track!" he yelled. "It's Milli Vanilli all over again!"

"That's my old friend, Mack," she chuckled. "We grew up together in Adams Morgan."

"Adams Morgan!" Mack roared. "Word up! Word up!"

"Y'know, we're both Dominican…"

"Dominican Republic! D-R! D-R!"

"This song goes out to him. 'Cause even though we have our

differences, community is important, y'know. Here goes." Ingrid's band launched into their song. She crashed and thrashed on her guitar, strangling the chords.

That sense of unreality came over Mack again, and he became aware of colors. Not actual color, but the *feeling* of color, the life and vibrancy that comes with it. He saw red and orange swirling like a whirlpool before his eyes. "The hell's wrong with me?" he panicked, heart racing, his mind reeling at these sudden visions. He hadn't gotten high today. Grabbing the arms of the people closest to him, he reached out for anything to anchor him in the real world. But the punks seemed possessed by the same hallucinations, grabbing their heads and yelling in confusion.

"What the fuck?" Mack gasped. Onstage, Ingrid played while her bandmates let their instruments slip from their hands, and Mack saw the visions streaming smoke-like from the strings of her guitar. Gritting his teeth, he tried to fight back, but they drew him like a fly to fresh meat. Gripped him and wouldn't let go, carrying him to a time before time. Mack surrendered and began to move, slowly, in a circle.

Mack saw—no, felt—the explosion. The force of a hundred million hydrogen bombs blasted him to atoms. From this destruction birthed creatures of immense beauty, pride and majesty. Hundreds of them. Capable of such benevolence their very presence eased his fears. So terrifying he wanted to grovel. Mack became one of them. Seeing through their eyes, trapped within their memories. He felt light as a bird, huge as a mountain. Beating his bat-like wings across the endless sea of stars, his spirit sang with the thrill of exploration. He had his whole life to explore this new universe, and he lived forever. Streaking faster than light, his thick mane ruffling, the stars blurring past him.

Through the visions, Mack became aware of the punks in the club moving in a circle, entranced just like him. Mack no longer cared, losing himself in the current.

The creatures visited every world, carried the knowledge they gained once those worlds became dust. Only on one planet did they find intelligent life. There they settled, so many they blotted the sky like a great churning stormcloud. The planet's young sun reflected off scales of gold, white, silver, green and black. Some breathed fire, others lightning; others breathed ice and great gales of rain. Many of them wanted to pass on their limitless knowledge to the beings of this world, who crawled from their caves like infants from the mother's womb. Others, made arrogant through their knowledge, looked at their new land as a place ripe for plunder. Who better than they to rule as overlords?

A thousand angry shrieks rent the skies. For seven days and seven nights the pitiful creatures of the earth waited for the gods to stop arguing. In the end, the wyrms split. Half flew toward the sunrise, half to sunset.

Mack and the punks broke into a run, holding onto each other's shoulders as they circled around. Ingrid's two bandmates dove into the pit, leaving her to play alone under the red phosphorescent lights.

Mack experienced the dream of imparting knowledge. The wyrms of sunset embarked into the human world. Knowing their true forms were too intimidating, they took guises to amaze. Butterfly wings, pointed ears and silken shapes. As one of them, Mack went among the people, dispensing the gift of reason. Fire sprouted in their caves, the crude rocks and sticks became tools. He gave the short, hairy creatures only enough knowledge to figure things out for themselves, watching them flourish like a proud father.

Abruptly, Mack found himself in a nightmare. Bloated lizards sat on mounds of treasure, presiding over blood sacrifice. Calling themselves Lords of the Earth, they gorged on the virgin daughters the puny short-lived apes offered as tribute. Thousands fell victim to the gluttony of the wyrms of sunrise. Mack gagged as the blood gushed between his teeth. He loathed himself for taking part in this greed. Gold and silver grew in heaps around him. Rubies trickled glittering between his claws. His whole life became for gold, so much he ignored the wings on the horizon.

Ingrid launched into a solo. Mack and the punks ran in an ever-widening circle. He experienced a million joys. He wailed under a million sorrows. Time moved on.

The world shook with war. The wyrms of sunrise thought their cousins weak, never expected the attack. Blood spilled from the skies like red rain. Lightning created daylight over the battlefields. Spiteful, those wyrms that breathed frost spread the winter of their wrath over the world. Mack, who was both a wyrm of sunrise *and* sunset, ran the gauntlet of emotion. He rejoiced in setting his enemies ablaze, watching their corpses plummet like shooting stars. He cried as his talons slashed open his cousins' sulfurous bellies, his tears falling to scorch the frozen earth.

The punks tripped and fell over each other, crashing to the floor. Within moments they were up again, running. Ingrid's guitar shrieked loud enough to blow the amplifiers.

In the end, the wyrms left a world covered in ice, and their once great race decimated. Mack felt indescribable sorrow, like he would never be happy again. Of the survivors, some huddled in their lairs amidst their treasure, nursing dying dreams of domination. Others curled up and slept eternally, letting forests and cities grow on their backs. Every few hundred years they had nightmares of the war and spewed forth flame in their fitful slumber, swallowing whole civilizations in molten destruction. The wyrms of sunset, who wished only to share their knowledge, found nothing but wretchedness in their victory.

Mack couldn't stop moving with the tide of birth, death, love and destruction.

The wyrms of sunset took human guise, planning to impart what remained of their wisdom. Ready to enter the humans' world, they did not count on their wicked cousins. The three remaining wyrms of sunrise, hidden for centuries in their cave, called a false truce. They said they had seen the error of their ways. When their cousins let their guard down, the three wyrms ambushed them. Fire engulfed Mack, burning him to cinders. Murdered, leaving only a memory of him for humans to base their legends.

The 9:30 Club had become a spinning wheel of humanity. Mack picked up a boy who'd been knocked down, threw a strong arm around his shoulder and continued running with him, the two of them banging their fists. Mack's green checkered vest was stained black with sweat.

The last six wyrms of sunset stood in a circle. One by one, they disappeared into the vessel that would carry their memories: six glittering strings. From their new home, they watched the Normans and Anglos rise to power. They saw endless wars rampage across the world. The Turks, the Romans, Napoleon, Hitler; they all rose and fell with the ebb of time. The old gods surrendered to the new god. Whether as harp, lute, violin, mandolin, sitar or guitar; they always found someone to pluck the strings. For a while their tale became known, as they wanted. Then their cousins found them.

Ingrid's voice rang out clear and beautiful over the din, like cathedral bells chiming in the midst of a hurricane. Eyes closed, neck veins bulging, she pressed her lips right on the microphone. She and the guitar worked together. It gave her the words, and she gave voice to their age-old song:

United, from the dawn of time we came
No regrets, no fear, no sense of time
United, we filled the stars with our rhyme
Divided, we mourn the dying of our flame

Mack's every breath was a struggle. He stank, as did everyone, and their collected smell overwhelmed any other stench in the club. Ingrid grimaced as she shredded on her guitar. Sweat pouring down her face, she looked like a woman locked in battle.

Movement at the back of the club caught Mack's attention through the haze of history, drew him back to the present. Icy dread gripped him. The skinheads had returned. The big one dumped the Yes-Men, now beaten unrecognizable, off his shoulders. Standing over the prone body of the ticket man, the tall one blew smoke out his nostrils. He no longer held a cigarette.

*Ingrid crouched in a dumpster that reeked of sour milk. Picking through an egg carton, she threw out the broken ones. Slimy yolk oozed onto her fingers. Hopefully there would be enough for tomorrow's omelet. She had twenty bucks to buy food, thanks to some generous lady who happened to leave her purse lying around. The dumpster sat on a sewer grating. Beneath her, a subway train rumbled down the track.*

*Low voices murmured in conversation at the other end of the alley. Quickly, she jumped out the dumpster and knelt behind it, heedless of the puddle water seeping through her jeans. Three skinheads emerged through the manhole steam, crunching broken glass under their boots. Ingrid always saw them at shows, guzzling 40s, danger wafting from them like a stink. Most drunk asshole punks didn't scare her, but these ones did. Something in their eyes: complete disdain and lack of remorse, like beating someone up was the least they could do.*

*They unlocked the door to an alley apartment and stepped inside. The tall one took a last look around before locking the door. His eyes never opened. Ingrid ran to the apartment. Her blood froze with the fear of being caught, but her curiosity outweighed fear every time. Standing on a trashcan, she peered through the window bars.*

*Light stabbed her eyes, almost blinding her. She marveled at the wonders inside the grimy apartment. The skinheads strolled contemptuously through the treasures of the ages. Spilling beer on ancient swords, blowing their noses on silk dresses, eating diamonds and spitting out the dust. Sitting in their thrones, they revealed their true form. Their faces stretched, becoming long and green, rows of fangs sprouting in their mouths. Ingrid stood paralyzed, fighting to keep her sanity. Resisting the urge to run screaming into the night and never stop running. This was wonder. This was horror. This was her dreams and nightmares all crammed in the roach-infested room.*

*The lizard-woman picked up a red guitar from the treasure pile, settled it across her soggy stomach and began to play. Her slender fingers plucked a beautiful melody from the six shining strings. The lizard-men swayed their necks like snakes under a charmer's spell. Ingrid saw what they saw, felt what they felt. Shades of long ago filled her vision, staggering her mind. The lizard-woman didn't finish the song, but cut herself off in the middle, and with a satisfied smile laid the guitar on the floor. Her last note rang in the silence, her companions still swaying their heads.*

*It took Ingrid long minutes to compose herself. Her gaze drew to the guitar lying amid the jewels. She heard whispery, gossamer voices in the air, telling her of an ancient injustice. A feeling of anger slowly replaced her stunned reverie. The bastards thought they had a right to all this just because they could breathe fire and shit?*

The skinheads made a beeline for Ingrid, crashing through the wall of punks like a bowling ball through tenpins. For that split second, Mack saw them in stomach-wrenching clarity: slavering tongues hanging out their mouths, faces twisted in bloodlust, completely unstoppable. Coming for Ingrid.

Without a second thought, Mack tackled the biggest one to the floor. Pain rippled through his body. He rained blows on the skinhead that would have caved in an average man's cheek. The skinhead slapped Mack hard enough to rattle his brain. Through the stars swirling before his eyes, he saw the big skinhead and the woman turn toward Ingrid. Grabbing their ankles, he held them back, gritting his teeth through their savage kicks. His face was on fire. The metallic taste of his own blood filled his mouth. He held on. Ingrid played on.

The tall one hopped onstage, eyes closed, smoke billowing out his nostrils and curling up around his ears. A serpentine grin played on his dagger-sharp face. Screaming, Ingrid almost dropped the guitar. Possessed with an uncanny strength, Mack ran onstage, picked up the tall one and hurled him down on top of the female. Just as quick, a pair of strong hands pulled him to the floor.

The big skinhead tried to close his blunt fingers on Mack's neck. Grabbing hold of his wrists, Mack struggled against the hands that inched closer, closer, to his throat. He could best any man in strength, but felt like a child in the grip of his massive attacker. Mack began to hallucinate the skinhead's face sagging like a dollar store mask. Neck swelling to twice the size of his head. Flames licking out between his sharp teeth. A string of drool fell from his mouth, landing on Mack's arm with a sizzle and blistering pain. Grunting, grinning, the skinhead pinned Mack's elbows under his knees, slowly pushed against Mack's wrists until he gripped his trachea. The fingers squeezed and Mack's lungs screamed in agony. He felt weightless. A floating, numb feeling, like he was dreaming. Or dying. Dimly, as if from a mile away, he heard Ingrid strike the last note and finish her song.

And then he was free. Gasping for breath, he sat up, shocked to see the three skinheads now ran in a circle. Frenzied, senseless, running to a song nobody heard but them.

Shadowy figures appeared above the stage. Their very presence dwarfed Mack in its grandeur. He became the tiniest ant, gawking at the six reptilian bodies made from the stuff of stars. Blazing with heat, their hearts glowed fire-red through their scaly breasts. They spoke in booming voices that could kill with a word. *Come home*, they said gently, with such love Mack knew he would never be able to describe it. No one moved, save the skinheads. They snaked their necks, mesmerized. Mack saw great starry wings stretch out, wrapping the skinheads in their embrace. In an instant, they all disappeared.

The punks looked about in confused silence, so quiet Mack could hear the hum of the amps. He'd have sworn the wyrms of sunset had never been there at all, were it not for the image of terrible, glorious love imprinted on his soul.

Ingrid fell to her knees. Mack ran onstage. Shivering and crying, she threw herself into his arms. "*No te preocupes, mi amor*," he said. The words came out, simple and true. "*No tengas miedo. Ya no están aqui.*"

"*No tengo miedo.*" She put her head on his chest. Giving a soft laugh, she pointed to the guitar. "*Están alli.*"

Mack left for California in the morning. A small group saw him off. His mother, smothering him in kisses. His brother. His two little sisters. Ingrid. Dressed in a corduroy jacket and ski cap, smiling up at him with her big smile. Still looking shaken from her ordeal, she handed him her prized guitar.

"I don't ever want to see it again," she told him. "They want it passed on. But I do want you to come back sometime." Gently, she touched his bruised face. He cupped her cheek in his palm. So dark, so lovely. Mack leaned in for a hug, and she kissed him in the falling snow.

Watching the mist-enshrouded pastures roll by along Interstate 76, Mack touched the slender strings of the guitar in his passenger seat. It had a new string, with a new story of how the last dragons joined their brethren after too long a separation. He would pass it on, as Ingrid asked. The memory of her soft lips lingered in his mind. Not a reflection of the past, but a promise for the future. That memory carried him state by state, mile by mile, towards the next journey.

OPEN

# WHEN THE LAW COME

"Well, I'll tell the story if you don't mine settin a spell. I know I don't mine gittin a chance to stretch these ole bones. Jest as long as you don't innerupt me, or say some nonsense. C'mon, I'll tell you bout that ole gen'ral stow. Wut? You heard that one already? Well, son, you gone hear it agin. I remember that stow. Those that been there allus miss it, and those that ain't been there miss it, though they ain't never seen o' heard bout it..."

### The Law Comes to Mister Cousins' General Store

The law came to Mister Cousins' gen'ral stow like a whisper through the wheat. Most folk slept quietly in they beds as it snuck cross the cornfields and stole up to that li'l shack that sat halfway between Birmin'ham and the land o' shadows. Only two folks wuz up: Not-Penelope, who never slept, but wuz even then cookin in her pantry, fingertips stained violet from the beets she wuz cuttin. And Remus wuz awake. By now Remus wuz ancient, but jest as hardy as he ever wuz.

"Jim?" Like the sharpest axe, his voice cut the still spring night. "Jim?" Runnin out his cabin, Remus called fo' his friend, but couldn't see him nowhar. The crescent moon hung overhead, a bone-white sliver peekin out through the dark. Grabbin his wheat sickle, Remus stood on that road and faced down the law. Like the Reaper hisself, he slashed at wut cain't be cut, stabbed at wut cain't die. He battled it with his big, rough hands that had wrestled lion-men and Louisiana mudsharks, and far fiercer things. Remus gave all he had, but the law came, and the law won.

When it left, couldn't nobody remember whether the gen'ral stow had stood at all. Folk drove by in they cars, and stopped. There they sat fo' minutes, sometimes hours, rackin they brains tryin'a remember why this patch o' overgrowed grass seemed so familiar. Fin'ly, they allus gave up and continued on they way.

## The Right Way To Worship

It came to be, sometime in the year nineteen twenty-three, when Jim wuz wukkin the gen'ral stow one morn. Jim wuz a good sort, a skinny-bone fella with gray sidewhiskers and his apron allus dusted in flour. He carried on him the stow's smell o' wheat and garlik, so's that evuhwhar he went he left a li'l scent o' stow. Niggers round them parts said Jim had wukked there a hunnerd years. You would guess he'd never been young at all.

In fact, he hadn't been. Many years ago, he burst forth full-growed, right in the middle o' the gen'ral stow, in a great sploshun o' fire. It wuz a feat he'd grown tired o' talkin bout, and, to evuhbody's disappointment, the ole clerk never came close to doin it agin.

He wuz stackin bags o' fertilizer when in come Miss Molly, all mad and fussed-like, draggin her son Jeremiah by the horns. Now, that boy wuz half-boy, half-bull: he had two giant horns curvin on top his head and hooves instead o' hands. They said his mama wuz right awful to a tree witch one day, so she put a hex on her that made her baby come out with horns and hooves. His face wuz red from cryin so hard.

"Mawnin, Miss Molly," sez Jim. "Wut'choo need t'day?"

"I don't know wut to git," she said, slappin the boy's behind. "This boy done embarrassed me at revival."

"Now wut did he do?" Jim ast, smilin at the li'l fella.

"When it came time to give praise," sez Molly, sez she, "this li'l heathen pulled down his pants. Then he starts gruntin like a pig. Then, in front o' the whole congregation, he takes a piss. Then he starts creepin round. But that ain't the end of it! He starts screamin and throwin things at evuhbody, jumps up and lands right in the mud. He embarrassed me in front o' Reverend Hawkins and the whole town! Lawd! Why wuz I cussed with such a wicked son?"

"Well," said Jim, "that is a right strange way to worship. Why don't you 'splain y'self, young man?"

The li'l half-bull boy sniffed, tuckin his cow-tail tween his legs. "That's how you give praise, I swar! I wuz jest doin wut Mister Young over by the creek tole me to do."

"Wut Mister Young tole you to do, huh?" Jim knew all about that sinner.

"I wuz fishin," said Jeremiah, "and I sees him walk up to that yallah lady's house, and knock on the doh' and take his pants off. Then he goes inside and he starts gruntin. Then he comes out and pees on a tree. I knows I shouldna been so curious, mama, but I followed him back to his cabin. He's creepin round, and Missus Young opens the doh' and starts throwin things at him, and she's screamin and hollerin. Then Mister Young runs away and falls right down in front o' me in the mud. Then he tells me that evuhthin I jess saw wuz how he and his friends give the glory, and I shouldn't tell nobody."

Jim laughed. "Boy, I don't think wut you saw wuz worshippin."

"But that's how you worship!" the boy insisted. "Cuz Missus Young got the spirit at revival. When I 'splained m'self to the reverend, I went to go talk to him by the Youngs, and when she heard me she started screamin and throwin things at Mister Young all over agin. So it must be the right way!"

## Remus Returns

All kinds'a folk used to come by Mister Cousins' gen'ral stow back in them days. There wuz them no-good harpies allus flyin round, pickin up travelers off the road and killin 'em; there wuz the Fates takin the yarn strands that wuz folks' lives and weavin 'em into quilts with they nimble fingers; the witch Ezra with her rattlin bracelets o' bone and silver; Beelzebub hisself would come to play cards. But Jim liked none of 'em better'n Remus.

Remus had jest escaped from Hell fo' the second time. He came into that gen'ral stow lookin like a dog done chewed him up, arms covered up to the elbows in blood (most o' which warn't his own). The blackbirds in the rafters cawed and flapped they wings at the sight o' him, rainin down feathers. When Remus sat, Jim saw the blood pourin from the cut on his cheek. Remus ast fo' coffee with extra milk. And when a man like him ast fo' extra milk, Jim damn well gave it to him. "How you doin?" Jim ast him. "You need anythin else?"

"Kin I ax a favor?" Remus sez.

"Anythin."

"Lemme use yo' well out back. I know yo' boss'll be plenty mad, but I gots to git cleaned up."

"Mister Cousins gone off to the bak'ry. He won't be back fo' while. Naw, take yo' time."

Remus smiled. "Thank you kindly. I'm goin wooin t'night!"

Jim scrunched up his face. "Addy May? *Agin?* Ain't she turned you down twice?" If Remus had a weakness, Addy May Brewster wuz it. Jess the thought of her hit him like the bourbon in a mint julep, makin him all swoony and stupid.

"That she has," sez Remus. "Twice she slammed the doh' in my face. And all the heroic deeds in the world don't mean nuthin to her. But I feel t'day's my lucky day."

"Well, you kin sho' use the well." And Remus did jess that, scrubbin off every last bit o' dirt and demon blood.

A week later, Jim heard Remus and Addy May wuz gittin married. He jest had to ax her when she came in the stow. "Tell me, Addy May: Wut made you change yo' mine?"

Addy May wuz pretty as a pitcher, and already looked a blushin bride with her flower basket. "It din't mean much to me when Remus came by talkin bout killin giants and the like," sez Addy May. "But I saw him come back on his way from Hell lookin all tow up. Then he came to my doh' that same day lookin like he ready fo' a high 'ciety party. I don't care much fo' great deeds, but any man who kin clean up that nice is a keeper."

## Why Alabama Has Winter Tornadoes

One winter, back when Remus wuz a younger man, he came to the gen'ral stow to see Brother Wind. Well, Remus went struttin right up to him like he owned the world and wuz out collectin rent from evuhbody in it. "I'ma challenge you, ole man!" sez Remus.

Brother Wind wuz older'n the ocean, with hair like a snow-capped peak and a whistle to his voice. "How, son?" he sez. "Wut kin you do that's better'n me?"

"I's a better dancer," sez Remus. Well, Brother Wind's eyes went wide like an owl's! Even ole Jim, who had seen a lot, couldn't believe wut he heard. Now, Brother Wind considered hisself the best dancer: he'd two-stepped all over the world. Every spring he wuz known to dance round the countryside. Seein fit to teach this upstart a lesson, he accepted the challenge.

Fo' days they danced cross the cornfields. Remus did all the ole steps, jump-up, step-back, and made a few new steps. A li'l shuffle, a li'l hop-jig long the Mi'sippy. Where Brother Wind danced, the land got stripped bare. Barns crushed flat neath his tappin feet. Cypress trees bent full back, and all the forest creechers ran fo' they lives. Whole towns blew away. Some folk even died. Even as they ran, no one could deny the beauty o' Brother Wind's dancin as he spun cross the farmland, jugglin lightnin and wearin black sky fo' a hat.

As the ole man got tired, he saw Remus had as much energy as ever, if not mo'. Nuthin could stop that Remus' longlegged hoppin. Brother Wind warn't bout to be outlasted. The sun rose and set sebben times befo', with a tired wheeze, the ole man collapsed right on his face, and that Remus kept right on leapin through the sunflowers. By then, the land had been tow up so bad it took half a year fo' Alabama folk to git things straight. All the ole ladies who wuz judgin the contest agreed Remus wuz a better dancer, and much classier in his presentation.

Brother Wind felt so vexed he came back every year round Thanksgiven, challengin Remus, dancin so hard the hills shook. City folk shut they windows o' packed up they belongins and ran. The folk round Mister Cousins' gen'ral stow knew it was jess Brother Wind showin off, and they paid it no mine. Remus ignored him completely. "A winner's a winner," he allus said.

### Aunt Rose and the Harpies

Well, it came bout time that Remus completed six o' the sebben tasks that ole sooth-sayer set befo' him. He lassoed the Mi'sippy; he caught a herd o' wild buffalo; he went down to Hell to prick the Devil's tail; he fetched the ole king's crown from the bottom o' Martin Lake; he wrestled the troll unner the bridge fo' a whole week til he won; he even outraced that demondog who lives up there in the foothills. His final task wuz fo' to fetch a harpy's egg from they nest. Now, them harpies caught word o' this, and they ain't like it one bit. So's all five of 'em came down from the hills to give Remus wut fo'.

A mile from the stow there lived Aunt Rose, a woman who wuz round like an apple. Aunt Rose wuz hangin her laundry outside her cabin, smokin a pipe and whistlin to herself, when she heard big feet flappin on the dusty road, and who come along but them harpies. Wings folded on they backs, they feathers wuz shinin silvery. Aunt Rose liked 'em bout as much as she liked yeast stickin to her fingers. "Howdy,Aunty," they shrieked at her.

Aunt Rose covered her ears. "I'll say howdy to y'all, too, but I'd rather y'all din't talk so loud."

Bein mean sorts, the harpies jess laughed. "We lookin fo' this nigger name o' Remus," they sez. "You know whar he be at?"

"And wut do y'all want with Remus?" she ast, mighty spishus.

"Look here, woman," one of 'em sez, "we's here to give him a thrashin. And if'n you don't tell his whar-bouts, we'll thrash you, too."

Aunt Rose felt right mizrable fo' a second, then she tole 'em: "He over by the creek."

"Thank you, ma'am," they sez, and they gave her thirty cents jest to rub it in, that she betrayed him and all. Aunt Rose gave it right back to 'em.

"Why you give us our money back?" they ast, mighty vexed.

"Fo' a coffee pot," she sez.

"Wut'choo mean?" they ast.

Aunt Rose laughed a big ole laugh. "I don't deserve that money, seein as I din't help you none. If anythin, I helped Remus, since now he don't gotta go look fo' y'all. Take that thirty cents and buy y'self a coffee pot. Cuz once Remus through wit'choo, that's all they'll need to bury you in, I swar to Gawd!"

## Aunt Rose and the Pastor

One day Aunt Rose got right fed up with her shiftless son Jason. All day long he'd lay in the barn, snoozin. So she goes to Reverend Hawkins, and she sez, "What am I gone do bout Jason? He twenty-five years ole and all he do is lay bout."

"Well," the pastor sez, "maybe he hasn't found his callin yet. Our savior din't start his ministry til he was thirty."

"I *knows* that," sez Aunt Rose. "The difference is, our savior wuz only *born* in the stable. After you reach a certain age, you gots to git out!"

## How Jason Fleeced the Landlord

Jason took over his pa's piece o' sharecrop land once the ole man passed. In doin so, he also took up his pa's debt to Mister Cousins fo' all the tools and fertilizer they used over the years. Jason wuz a lazy sort, and din't much care fo' no one but hisself. He allus figgered his lucky break wuz waitin for him, like a ripe peach ready to fall off the branch into his hands.

Back bout nineteen fo'ty-six there wuz a bad crop. Still, Jason had to hitch up the wagon to go give half of it to the landlord, Mister Sims. He took the long way round through the woods, seein as how harpies wuz harryin folk on the main road, and down by the river the lion-men wuz feudin with Black Crow Injuns. While drivin that wagon, Jason saw a tree witch lyin in the road. He reached fo' his double-barrel, but saw she warn't no threat. Not carin a whit fo' her, he tried to drive round, but this witch wuz a long woman and blocked the whole path.

"Help me," sez the witch. "I feel so weak. While I wuz sleep, someone took me out my tree and left me here. Take me back, so I kin have my powers agin."

With a groan, Jason picked up that long ole witch and took her to the woods; deep in the swamp, whar the witches flew, black skirts flut'rin, through the green vapors. It wuz fall, and the oaks whar them witches lived looked like some giant had took a bite from they boughs.

Jason helped the witch climb back in the branches. “Thank you, young man,” sez the witch. “Fo’ yo’ kindness, I’ma give you this fleece.” And she dropped a dirty sheepskin full o’ flies right in front o’ him.

“Mmm…Thanks,” sez Jason. You cain’t refuse nuthin from a witch once she gives it to you. So’s he went back to the path, threw that fleece on his mule, and all of a sudden that mule turned into a purr-bread mustang!

“Good Lawd!” he sez. “I sho’ is lucky with this magic fleece, here.” He put the fleece on the crop, and now he had enough pumkin and corn and squash to last the winter. Jason couldn’t believe his luck. With his new hoss, he kept on down the road to give the landlord his half.

Jason stopped at the gen’ral stow to see Mister Cousins, who he owed so much money. On the way in, he saw Remus carryin the bodies o’ two harpies he done kilt. He wuz gone bury ‘em and pay proper respeks, holdin ‘em like they wuz babies made o’ glass. “I’ma pay off my debts,” Jason proudly tole Remus. And Remus jess gave him a smile.

Mister Cousins liked to turn into a blackbird and fly round the stow, and cuz o’ this his face allus looked a li’l beakish. Jason took out wut change wuz in his pocket, dropped it on the counter, put the fleece over it, and when he took it off he had fifty dollars.

“Mebbe that kin pay off my family’s debt some,” he sez, and Mister Cousins’ eyes bout popped out his head. Jim whistled at Jason’s good fortune. Happy as a cat in milk, Jason rode his new hoss to the landlord’s, dropped off his half and went home.

Usin the fleece, Jason doubled wut he grew fo’ his next crop. Then he sold it, and boy! He made enough money to buy his own plot o’ land, with a nice big cabin on it. After while, his landlord Mister Sims learnt bout wut Jason done with his fleece. Well, he warn’t much fo’ lettin niggers have sum’n so nice, not when he wanted it fo’ hisself. He dreamt o’ keepin it and becomin rich, like them plantation owners in Mobile. So’s he went to see Jason at his cabin, and he sez: “You see here, nigger! Half o’ wut you got is mine. So I want that fleece right now!”

“Suh,” sez Jason, “I wants to show you sum’n.” He took Mister Sims out to the stables, pointed to his mustang. “Y’see that hoss? Right now he’s eatin wut I picked from my garden t’day. Now, I reckon in a few hours bout half o' that's gone come out his rear end. And you kin keep that, Mister Sims, cuz that's the last half you gone git from me!"

## Jason and the Pastor

With his magic fleece, Jason became the most successful colored man in town. He married well, and had a daughter name o' Penelope. He built a cabin fo' his mama to spend her ole age. He even bought a brand-new Buick.

In them days, niggers got strung up fo' less uppity behavior than Jason wuz showin, but white folk like Mister Cousins knew better. The one time crackers tried to hang a nigger round the gen'ral stow, Remus sent 'em flyin so far they woke up in Georgia.

After all that prosperity, Jason started sinnin. Reverend Hawkins got tired o' his puttin on airs. One night, the reverend relaxed in his favorite chair, the taste o' his wife's pork still on his tongue, but all he could think bout wuz Jason's smug ole face. Throwin on his coat, he went right to Jason's house to tell him wut's wut.

"Jason!" he called, bangin on the doh'. "I'm gittin tired o' yo' backslidin. You allus gittin drunk and duckin on yo' Gawd-blessed wife with them loose gals. Every time you sin, you allus come to revival cryin, and we allus forgive you, then you go and sin agin. I got a right mind to kick you out the chu'ch. Jason! Open yo' doh'!"

The doh' creaked open, and there stood Jason, cryin like a baby. "I din't mean to do it! I don't know wut I wuz thinkin!"

"Jason," sez the reverend, dread scuttlin cross his spine, "wut you do?"

"I jest wanted to make her prettier," cried Jason. "Kin you change her back? Lawd, please change her back!"

They went into the big family room. Instead o' Jason's li'l pigtailed Penelope in the overstuffed armchair, there sat a full-growed young woman. She wuz stunnin, achin beautiful and dark-skinned, lookin at 'em with hazel eyes shaped like teardrops. But she warn't Jason's daughter. She wuz someone completely different. Jason fell in the reverend's arms, weepin. And from then on he locked that fleece up and never touched it agin.

## Not-Penelope

Jason called the changelin Not-Penelope. This gal wuz evuhthin Jason wanted when he used that fleece, but in a way he couldn't unnerstand. She wuz brown as an acorn, from the top o' her hair to her tiny, perfik feet. She had a voice like water tricklin over mossy stones, but only spoke when she had to. This long gal moved dainty-like, and her smile curved at the ends, and her hands wuz stovepipe-hot to the touch. Instead o' goin to chu'ch, she spent time listenin to tree witches, absorbin they teachins like a flower absorbs sunlight. Not-Penelope already knew how to clean and cook; she din't need nobody's help and din't ask fo' none.

Jason grew 'fraid o' Not-Penelope. Her eyes wuz hazel mirrors, and every time he looked in 'em he saw hisself, small and gaunt. Sometimes he grew so 'fraid he beat her, but she never cried. When folk came over to see him, they wunnered whar Jason went off to, only to find he'd been there all along, quiet as a ghost in his own family room, while from the pantry they heard the steady sound o' Not-Penelope scrapin pans clean.

Most folk expected to one day wake up and find Not-Penelope gone, flown off like a bird in spring. Mebbe she might have, if it warn't fo' the day she wuz walkin through the woods, tripped and fell right in a giant briar patch. Hurtin from all the scratches, she looked up to find she wuz in a maze o' thorns, the branches like high walls, the thorns theyselves long as a man's arm and proddin her like spears.

Not-Penelope mighta found her way out that briar maze; she had instinks most other folks din't. But, with them same instinks, she sensed someone else in there, and followed the feelin o' melancholy as she wound her way through the maze. The full moon wuz a beacon in the sky by the time she reached the center, whar she saw Jeremiah Half-Bull sittin statue-still on a bench.

"Oh!" He looked up in surprise. "Not-Penelope! Wut is you doin here?"

"I don't know," she said. "I do wut I do. Other people discuss why

I do it."

The half-bull, half-man tried to brush off his overalls, but couldn't hide the fact he'd been wukkin the fields. "Well, I come here sometimes jest to git away from things." He patted his hoof on the seat beside him. "Would you mine settin? Even if you gotta leave, it'd be good to have yo' company jest a li'l while." To him, she looked like she jess stepped out a sweet dream. Seein her in his secret place—the queenly way she wore the moonlight as it bathed her top to bottom—gave him a courage he hardly never found round wimmen.

Not-Penelope gave him that witchy smile, cuz she knew she'd found a truly gentle soul. She took a seat beside him and watched the stars awhile. From then on, they met in the briar patch every evenin. In time they married, and had a smat'rin o' chilluns, with horns like they daddy and they mama's glidin step.

### The Beginning of the World

December came round, and Ole Man Winter come marchin through, turnin the cornfields to a forest of ice. As they did every year, a group came up from the land o' shadows: folk havin no color, neither man nor woman, movin they shapeless bodies through the pasture. Cross the cane and corn they went, pickin sunshine off the leaves, puttin the light in they satchels fo' when they went home. When they walked, all the farmers stayed indoh's, and even the folk in Birmin'ham felt a chill they couldna said wuz entirely from the cold.

Jim sat playin cards with two young'uns inside the gen'ral stow. One wuz Jeremiah Half-Bull, the other wuz this half-harpy boy from up in the hills. The Devil wuz there doin a li'l shoppin, but he din't join in the game; bein a lordly type, he hardly never played with common negroes. "Lemme tell y'all bout the beginnin o' the world," Jim sez.

"There wuz two god brothers walkin round the heavens. And between 'em they had jest one mule. And these brothers needed to git from one star to the other. The one brother, name o' Desire, sez if they jest push the mule they kin make it in time. The other brother, Law, wanted to rest the mule and make it some hoss-shoes from star stuff, thinkin that would make the ride easier. Well, they argued bout this fo' ages, til the two decided to jess split up.

"Law made one world. In that world, the people had control o' evuhthin that's possible. They could learn all the secrets o' the universe if they jest wukked and studied. The problem wuz, they'd never be satisfied, allus dreamin o' things they cain't see.

"Desire made a world whar people controlled the *im*possible. They could wave a hand and make dreams come true. They called it magic. The problem wuz, it's real dangerous to live somewhar anythin kin happen. Folk wuz allus livin in fear o' wut some magic person might do.

"Desire had to stay in his own world, and his brother in his. Two worlds, and never will one meet the other. That's the law."

"His brother found ways round that, though," said Jeremiah Half-Bull.

"That the law don't know bout," said the half-harpy boy.

"Yep," Jim said. "All over a mule." And he emptied his pipe ash in the spittoon.

## Aunt Rose's Sewing Circle

It came to be the middle o' the nineteen-fifties, and Aunt Rose, now goin on a hunnerd years ole, took a walk round the fields like she did now and then. A plane flew overhead, trailin exhaust so thick it looked like a white bridge cross the sky, and Aunt Rose could only shake her head at all these things she could never unnerstand. Why would you wanna fly when you got two good feet?

"Ain't you Jason's mama?" ast a rickety voice. She saw the Fates sittin on they porch: two ole wimmen, with skin like clay left to harden in the sun. One of 'em spun threads on her loom, the other measured 'em.

"Y'all got sum'n to say bout Jason, you better come out and say it," sez Aunt Rose, givin 'em a look harder'n day-ole biscuits. She well knew Jason warn't perfik, but she grew tired o' folk gittin in his business.

"Now, calm down, Sister Rose," said the one doin the measurin, name o' Lacky. "We's jess bein frenly."

"Ain't there s'posed to be three o' y'all?" ast Aunt Rose. She tried not to look at the strings, figgerin she had no right knowin how long someone's life wuz.

"Our sister Atta retired," said Clotho, the spinnin one. "Moved in with her son. Lacky been weavin the quilt and cuttin the threads, but it's a lotta wuk to do all that."

Aunt Rose took a look at they quilt o' evuh-changin patterns: a millyun tiny fibers wove into a blanket so big it took up the whole porch. Sometimes the threads wuz the color o' milk, and sometimes they wuz so bright you couldn't look at 'em. She saw the pitcher on the quilt shift from a cabin in winter to cowboys shootin at Injuns to white folks drinkin wine at a fancy party. Every few seconds a new image appeared, jest as dazzlin as the last. Lovely as it wuz, she couldn't deny it looked a li'l shabby with all them loose threads.

"Let me help," sez Aunt Rose, takin a seat in the empty rockin chair, pickin up the sewin needles. If you gone make a quilt outta folks' lives, she figgered, you better do it right.

So Aunt Rose, in her ole age, became one o' the Fates, jess like she somehow knew she would. Her grandchilluns and great-grandchilluns loved to sit round her as she wove that quilt from folks' life-threads. Fo' every thread they sewed in, she removed another. You could hear a sigh whenever she pulled it out and cut it with her rusty scissors.

## The Devil and the Twins

There wuz two twins by the name o' Freeman. One of 'em wuz cop'ry, like he jess stepped off a penny, and the other wuz shiny-black. Other'n that, they talked the same, dressed the same. They mighta been the same person and din't even know it.

One day the copper one came home cryin. "I done it this time!" he cries to his brother. "I lost my soul to the Devil in a card game." And he fell on the flow, screamin.

Well, the black one warn't gone see his brother in no pain. He went straight to that gen'ral stow, where Beelzebub sat playin cards with Mister Cousins and Ole Man Winter.

“Wut’choo up to, you?” ast the Devil. “You wanna play some cards?”

“You bastard!” sez Freeman. “You took my brother’s soul!” And he balled his fists, ready to punch Beelzebub.

Lucifer looked him up and down, impressed. “Oh, so you came to fight, huh?”

“If I has to. You took his soul, and now he cain’t git to Heaven.”

“Nigger,” sez the Devil, “wut makes you think he woulda gone to Heaven anyway? Evuhbody jest assumes they’ll get there, like it’s a done deal. I like yo’ gumption, son, but fightin me ain’t a good idea.”

“Cain’t you at least shorten the time he’ll spend in Hell? If you do, I’ll wuk fo’ you. I’ll bring half o’ my crops every harvest, after I’s done with my landlord’s half.”

“You’d do that?” sez Lucifer. “Son, even if I wanted to do wut you s’jest, I cain’t. There ain’t no such thing as time in Hell, so I sho’ cain’t add o’ take away from it.”

“Fine!” sez Freeman. “I’ll play you! If I win, I gits the soul. If you win, you gits mine’s, too. Double o’ nuthin!”

Ole Scratch thought a moment at this show o’ brotherly fekshun. Now, he allus wuz a gamblin man. If they played, he had no doubt he’d win. No man born o’ woman could beat him at cards. But Brother Freeman wuz earnest, and the Devil wuz swayed.

“I’ma make you a deal,” sez the Devil. “I’ll give you the soul. Thing is, you cain’t give it back to yo’ brother. It’s yours. Yo’ ‘sponsibilty. Yo’ brother has to go through life thinkin he damned. And if it gits lost o’ destroyed, that’s yo’ fault. You hold onto that soul, and when you o’ he dies it’ll go back to him.”

With that, Beelzebub grabbed a mason jar from the stow and put the soul inside. The soul still sits there in Mister Freeman’s cupboard, by the jars o’ honey and jam. He still ain’t tole his brother he has it, though he’s got it labeled SOUL so no one tries to spread it on toast by mistake.

## Stay Positive

Sister Autumn settled in, spreadin her skirts o' russet and gold over the land, and Remus moved his creaky bones to the stow fo' to buy some bread. "How you holdin up?" Jim ast him while he cleaned the shelves, as if he din't know every thought in Remus' head.

Now, Remus allus had the power o' Talkin. That's how he won so many fights. If you wuz in his way, he'd sing plantation songs til you couldn't think fo' y'self no mo' and you'd do whatever he sez. When he got mad, his voice could knock down small hills. And if you really annoyed him, he'd start spoutin so many stories bout foxes and rabbits and terrapins yo' mine would go mushy. That din't stop him from takin his blows. It had been ten years since he defeated the Swamp Lawd, bringin peace to the countryside, and the scars on his wrinkled face showed every battle.

"It's hard," sez Remus. "Some days I feel good, some days I feel like Jesus callin me. And Addy May's still gittin over that sickness. But I feel grateful. Every day I see my grandchilluns I feel grateful. You gotta be positive."

"Amen to that." Jim din't wanna worry his friend no way, but he felt he had to say sum'n. "Remus, I heard there's a young harpy comin fo' you. He sez you murdered his daddy and granddaddy."

"And prob'ly his great-granddaddy!" sez Remus. "I ain't up fo' no long fight. I figger I'll jess toss him in the river and drown him." And Remus threw his arms wide. "No worries. Hey, does that TV wuk?"

"Nope," sez Jim, tuggin on its rabbit-ears. "I wish it did. I wanna watch that ballgame t'night."

"It's no big deal."

"I tell you though," said Jim, "Mobile's team ain't lookin too good."

"They in a rebuildin season," Remus snapped at him. "Let's not talk like that. I wanna stay positive, now."

"Alright. I's jess sayin, they…"

"There you go agin, tryin'a upset me when I'm in such a good mood!"

"But—"

“Naw, nigger! Don’t you got wuk to do? Take that somewhar else, if you gone be negative.”

With a sigh, Jim went back to dustin shelves. “I wuz gone tell him that harpies kin swim,” he sez to hisself, “but since we stayin positive I best keep my mouth shut.”

## When the Law Came

The law came fo’ the gen’ral stow cuz it warn’t s’posed to be there in the first place. On that night, Not-Penelope looked up from her well-worn cuttin board, noticed the law, and kept choppin jest as she pleased. It came quiet as an indrawn breath, but that sound had Remus up and on full alert.

Steppin outside, he looked round fo’ the cause o’ his dread: at the land o’ shadows, and the crabapple trees, and the fields and the red-brick path to Hell. He din’t see the law til it wuz on him. Remus planted hisself in front o’ that law, and went at it with scythe and shotgun. But he fell, along with the stow and evuhthin round it.

In the morn, a roadwork crew set up they orange cones, and set to fixin a power line that fell. The colored chilluns walked a mile to they schoolhouse. George Wallace won his guvner campaign. Police hosed niggers down the street and sicked German Shepherds on chilluns, fillin the streets with screams and terror.

Sometime durin that, o’ maybe after, a man came fallin out a hole in the air. Buck nekkid, he brushed the fire out his hair, took a look at the swayin corn. A great laugh burst from his throat. He stepped onto the gen’ral stow porch, and there he sat, quiet-like, bidin his time til wuk, makin cabins and farms with his thoughts, and people to live in them cabins and farms, and dreamed up they tales as he wove straw from the sunlight.

# DEAD TEENAGERS

"Like, somebody always dies on Devil's Night," Tracy said. They stood on the steps of the Covington Library, which had closed for the night. Skateboarder kids did tricks off the handicap ramp. In the distance, Mindy saw the lights of Cincinnati glowing across the Ohio River. She slid a hand under Tracy's shirt and stroked his back, unable to shake a sense of foreboding. Whispers, bits of gossip she knew she shouldn't care about, but they lingered in her mind like a slow poison.

Mindy wore her Marilyn Manson shirt and bluejeans. Band names covered every inch of her black jacket: The Smiths, the Cure, Nine Inch Nails, Green Day, Depeche Mode, Siouxsie and the Banshees. She twirled a lock of hair around her finger, hair that she'd teased and buttered and hot-ironed until it was long and straight like a white girl's. She listened to a Korn song on her Discman.

Tracy wore his Halloween costume. Black pants and trenchcoat, a long black wig over his afro, white facepaint, black makeup around his eyes and mouth, a paper mache crow safety-pinned to his shoulder. He continued with his morbid topic. "Suicide, car crashes, ODs. Somebody always dies. And, like, the ghosts of kids who die come to kill other kids. If you're walking alone on Devil's Night, the ghosts will come get you."

"How do they kill you?"

"Fucking, I think. Like a succubus."

"I don't know what I'd do if I met a ghost," Mindy said. "I'd probably just be like, 'Hey, what's up, ghost? How ya doin'?' I'd probably scare him away."

"You scare *everybody* away." He chuckled, then turned serious. "A succubus is the worst kind of ghost. They spend eternity just feeding off people's life force. Since they have no feelings, they can't even enjoy the feeding. And they're, like, haunted by the stuff they did in life. Or if they die young, they're haunted by the things they *didn't* do. They take disguises to lure people in, and sometimes forget they're actually dead.

But they always remember, and it's like dying all over again."

Mindy shivered at the thought. "That sounds terrible."

Tracy shook his head. "When I die, I hope I'm just dead. Anything else…" He let the sentence trail off. "You still haven't told me what you're going as for Halloween." He gave her that charmingly crooked grin. "Halloween. Also known as: Mindy Day." They both laughed. "C'mon, what's your costume?"

"Okay, but don't tell anybody. For Mindy Day, I'm going as Dracula!"

"Are you a sexy Dracula?" Tracy asked hopefully.

"Oh no. So many girls do the sexy thing. Sexy vampire. Sexy angel. Sexy devil. Sexy insurance salesman. Sexy lunch lady. Andrea can pull off the sexy thing. I'm afraid I'd damage people's retinas."

"No," Mindy continued, "I'm doing total old school fucking Transylvania Count Dracula. I *love* vampire movies! I can do all the Draculas. Max Shreck." She skulked with feral shiftiness. "Bela Legosi." She regarded him with cold aristocratic arrogance. "Jack Palance." She bared her teeth with the promise of ultra-violence. "Christopher Lee." She gave him a leer of sexual menace. "Gary Oldman." She dropped to her knees and wailed melodramatically.

Tracy pulled her to her feet. "What're you listening to on your headphones? Korn? Why do you like them? Can't you listen to Children of Bodom, or Cradle of Filth?"

"I like Cradle of Filth," Mindy insisted. "Look, I know Korn's too mainstream for you, but, I dunno, I just like 'em. I think this song's about, like, strangling his wife." She did the Macarena dance, singing along. "*Your throat, I take grasp/And your eyes roll back/Love racing through my veins/Your heart stops beating…*"

Tracy held her against him. His trenchcoat felt warm as a blanket and his peachfuzz tickled her lips. Their tongues drew closer like magnets. Mindy slid hers along his, tasting his hot breath, touching the familiar parts of his body. Jutting hipbones. Arching back. Sharp shoulders. Wiry arms.

"You're so cute!" she gushed, putting her head on his chest, feeling his heartbeat flutter against her cheek. Mindy had gone further with him than with any other boy. It wasn't so bad, the fleshy taste of his cock as it fattened in her lips. She tried her best to make it sexy and fun, though his scraggly pubic hairs caught in her teeth and he came on her cheek. Mindy just licked the salty pearl off her face and smiled. The thought of losing him knotted her stomach, making her clutch him tighter. They made out for ten minutes. She caressed his upper leg, dangerously close to the crotch.

"Man, you big pimpin' already, Tracy?" said a nasal voice. "Aww fuck!" Mindy cringed. Her oldest memories of Zack Epstein involved him yelling at her in sixth grade tech crew about how she had no idea how to make a styrofoam star. A scrawny boy with a scraggly goatee and a shirt that said "I killed Kenny," spiky hair, acne like a topographical map on his face. Tracy only hung out with him because he had weed.

Two kids followed him, one of them Andrea. She had always been pretty, with billowy blond hair and pouty lips, but Mindy wasn't prepared for the knockout before her. Andrea had traded sweatshirts and ripped jeans for a black tank top and short skirt that fit like saran wrap over her deep cleavage and Barbie doll legs. Mindy felt like they existed in two different dimensions: her own body flat as a coin, Andrea exploding from her dress in full 3-D.

Swallowing her unease, Mindy embraced Andrea. "Oh, look at you! You're so hot!" Mindy wrinkled her nose at the smell of Andrea's perfume. She reeked of white roses.

Andrea smiled shyly, braces shining on her teeth. "It's the dress for my witch costume. You know, sometimes you want to wear something girly and cute." She had a musical Southern accent; a soft, purring quality to her cynical deadpan.

"I'll have your cape done by tomorrow," said Mindy. "I'm still sewing." She turned to the other kid, a new boy. Small, blond and pretty as a girl, he carried a red plastic double-sided lightsaber. "Are you gay?"

"No," he said, smiling.

"Can I tell people you're gay?"

The boy blushed red as a candy apple.

"I know I'm really forward. Trust me, you'll get used to it. You're so *cute!* You should dress as a schoolgirl for Halloween. What're you going as? Darth Maul? Fuck that *Star Wars* shit. You're going as a cute goth schoolgirl. Oh, hi, by the way! I'm Mindy."

"I apologize for her behavior," said Tracy. "She's always like this." He turned to Andrea, desire all over his face. "You're so sexy!" He grabbed her ass and kissed her deep.

For a month, Mindy and Andrea had shared Tracy. Spitting in the face of normal relationships, they both went on dates with him, both made out with him in the hallways. Andrea had been shocked when Mindy told her about the blowjob. After all, she hadn't really done anything with Tracy yet. Looking at Tracy making out with his sexy witch, Mindy wondered how long that would last.

"I need a hug," Mindy said. She embraced Epstein, then the blond boy.

Tracy broke the kiss, kept his arms around Andrea's waist. "I was just telling Mindy about the ghosts that come out on Devil's Night. Like, dead kids come and steal people's life force. Like a succubus."

"A what?" said Epstein. "A suck-my-dick?"

"That's not a succubus," said Andrea. "You're thinking about an *incubus*."

"I like Incubus," said Mindy, referring to the band.

"Nobody died last year," Andrea pointed out.

"Maybe this year somebody'll pull a Columbine," said Epstein. "Just walk up to where the preps hang out and mow down those motherfuckers." He glanced at Tracy as if looking for approval. Mindy wanted to point out that those kids were Nazis, and why would anybody want to be like them, but it didn't seem like the right time.

"God, Columbine was so dumb," Andrea said. "Everybody got all weepy, like it was the first time anybody ever died. Those kids would… have…died…anyway. It's not fucking important, people."

Mindy didn't like it when Andrea said things like that. A part of her envied the Columbine kids she saw on TV, laying wreaths and giving eulogies for dead friends. Caught up in Important Things. Matters of Life and Death. But then she started thinking about death, and felt small, the world shrinking until it swallowed her. It woke her up at night, screaming in horror.

“I’m bored,” said Tracy. “Let’s go.” Mindy took his one hand, Andrea the other, and they set off down the cracked sidewalk. Past the auto shops and bars of their lifeless town. Just as they started crossing the street, a pickup truck with a Confederate flag on the antenna sped toward them. Tracy yanked both girls back on the curb. A shaggy dog and a shaggy man glared out the window.

“Fucking Columbine kids!” the man yelled as he passed. Tracy gave him the finger.

“Fucking redneck!” he yelled. “I feel sorry for your dog!”

Mindy felt so brave when she was around Tracy. He responded to Columbine by fighting back, becoming more goth than ever. In the middle of lunch period, he argued with the vice-principal over his right to wear a studded collar. He had a witty retort for every prep who asked if he was in the Trenchcoat Mafia. Holding hands, the three of them flaunted their relationship to the Covington residents.

“I’m Andrea,” Andrea said in a husky, seductive voice.

“And *Iiiiiiii’m* Mindy!”

“And we are the Mistresses of Death.” Her arm around Mindy, Andrea fixed Tracy’s disposable camera with a gaze of nocturnal despair. Mindy licked the plastic scythe. Tracy took the picture. With a quick motion, Andrea drew the scythe across Mindy’s throat.

Mindy grabbed her neck, rolled on the ground. “Ack! Ack! I’m dying!”

Andrea nudged her with her foot. “You know you ruin it when you do that.” Mindy smiled.

They posed in front of a tombstone: “Alma Jane Heder. 1870-1883.” The kids sat around the ancient stones, smoking Camels and swigging from a bottle of gin Epstein swiped from his dad. The blond boy busily prepared their eggs and toilet paper.

Andrea licked imaginary blood off her fingertips. “Tastes delicious.”

“Your mom tastes delicious,” said Tracy.

“My mom’s a fucking bitch.”

“I love your mom,” said Mindy, standing up. “She has Lego hair. Do you know how Lego people have, like, that really square hair? Her mom has hair like that. This one time I was sleeping over Andrea's without permission, Misses Rukk comes downstairs and I hide under the bed. And she's got that green goo on her face and her brown roots are showing and she's like, 'Andiiiie? Is anybody with you, Andiiiie?'"

"God, you sound just like her," Andrea groaned. Mindy munched a bag of candy corn, let her friends take handfuls. Standing on her toes, Andrea kissed Tracy. Her shirt slid up, revealing a crescent of white stomach.

Epstein knelt in front of the tombstone. "Eighteen seventy to eighteen eighty-three? This kid died, like, a hundred years ago."

"Can you not be all on the graves?" said Tracy. "It's, like, disrespectful and shit."

"Who cares?" said Andrea. "It's not like they're gonna be any less dead."

"I just don't want them to come back as a succubus and fuck us to death," said Tracy. Mindy heard the anxiety under his laughter.

Epstein humped the tombstone. "Oh, yeah! Oh, baby! Necrophilia!"

"Fucking stop that!" They all backed away at Tracy's yell. An awkward silence followed, so tense Mindy just had to break it with a song and dance:

One day I ran
Into a man
And I asked, 'Why are you all made of bones?'
He said, 'It's easy to see!
I live in the cemetery!
That…is…my…home!'

"You have fucking ADD," said Epstein. "Not the first girl with ADD you've dated, huh, Trace?" Why in the hell did Epstein care so much about another boy's love life? Mindy wanted to push him in a mausoleum and lock it.

"Ta-da!" Tracy opened his trenchcoat and Mindy's breath caught in her throat. He had enough fireworks in his pockets to make the front page of every newspaper in the country. *Another Columbine?* they would cryptically say.

"We're gonna fuck shit up," Tracy said. "I'm gonna fuckin' dive in, throw fuckin' eggs and dive out like fuckin' Batman."

"Batman's a comic book," said Andrea. "It's not real."

"It would be so weird if real life was like Batman," Mindy mused, twirling her hair like she always did when nervous. "I mean, if there was, like, an evil clown killing people. And some dude whose face is all messed up, and one half of him's good and the other half's bad. If I saw that in real life, I'd be like, 'What the fuck? This is *crazy!*' Like, if you walked in your living room and there's a little guy wobbling around, like, 'Wobble wobble wobble! I'm the Penguin!' It'd be *crazy*. Then some dude dressed as a bat…"

Tracy gripped her shoulders. "Mindy, it's okay. Chill out." She pressed her forehead against his, closed her eyes. He kissed her, left her standing there while he went with Andrea.

"ARE...YOU...READY?" Epstein screamed in Mindy's ear. "Awwww fuck!" He shoved two pumpkins in her arms. She followed close behind Tracy and Andrea. They whispered to one another. Private jokes that made Andrea crack a smile. Mindy thought about all the things Tracy and Andrea could do when alone.

First, the teenagers walked to their high school and attacked it with zeal, flinging eggs at the double doors and the hated classroom windows. From there, they went back to Covington's main drag and lobbed pumpkins on the street, laughing as they exploded. They hid in an alley to watch the cars swerve around the orange pulp.

Tracy led them to an area of town filled with trailer homes. Children's toys and rusted car parts lay in the overgrown lawns. The goths stayed on each street just long enough to find a deserted-looking house, splatter every window, smash every pumpkin, drape every tree in TP, then run to the next street. The blond boy wore a huge grin the whole time. Mindy egged houses right alongside Tracy, but he didn't seem to notice. Andrea stood back, smoking a cigarette and tapping her feet. After every barrage, Tracy went back to her for his "power-up" kiss.

"Aww fuck!" crowed Epstein, wearing a Bill Clinton mask. Mindy looked in a car window at her hair falling in unruly tangles like a Medusa. Desperately, she tried to straighten it with her hands.

"Here," said Andrea, coming up behind her, pulling her hair in a ponytail and wrapping it with a tie. "There you go. You look great, Mindy." Mindy saw Andrea's face reflected in the window. Her friend smiled, showing two rows of small teeth usually caged behind her scowl.

They came to a quiet, dark trailer home. An electric sign in the window read JESUS SAVES in neon-blue like a porn shop sign. A Confederate flag hung off the antenna of the pickup parked outside. "That's the fucker who almost ran us over," sneered Tracy. "Fucking redneck and his stupid fucking redneck flag. Hold on. I need a re-charge." He kissed Andrea. Quickly, Mindy gave him a kiss, too. Reaching in his coat, Tracy pulled out a firecracker, lit it. "Let's see how he likes not having a mailbox."

The hissing fuse rained sparks on the gravel. "Tracy!" Mindy cried. "Please stop!"

"This isn't funny!" said Andrea.

"Blow that shit up!" said Epstein.

"Shut up, Epstein!" they both said.

Tracy lit three more firecrackers, dashed for the mailbox. Mindy held her breath. Just as he prepared to toss them in, a woman in curlers appeared on the front porch.

"Hey! What're y'all doin'?"

"OH SHIT!" yelled Tracy. Hauling his arm back like a soldier in the trenches, he hurled the firecrackers right at the woman. They burst on the stoop, spraying sparks around her feet. Screaming, she flung herself to the ground. Tracy stared dumbfounded, like he couldn't believe what he just did. From inside the house, they heard the unmistakable sound of a shotgun cock.

"Run, you fuckers!" Tracy grabbed both the girls' hands. All five kids ran far and fast, and didn't stop running until they reached the cemetery. Covered in sweat, Tracy dropped against a tombstone. His black wig frayed; his makeup streaked, creating brown stripes down his white face. He reminded Mindy of Neo from *The Matrix*. Heroic techno music played in her head as he stood up, disheveled and sexy.

She reminded herself she was mad at him.

"Tracy!" roared Epstein. "The pimpinest kid in Covington!"

Tracy grinned at Mindy, sweat dripping into his teeth. "Let me have some candy corn," he panted.

Mindy dumped it on the ground. "Go get it."

"I need some weed after that," Epstein said, like he'd actually done something. He pulled a bag out his pocket.

"Let me roll it," Andrea offered.

"Yeah right, like you know how. Back off!"

"Can I at least look at it? I want to make sure it's good."

"My penis is good."

Tracy took Mindy's hand. Her anger forgotten, she followed him under the overhanging branches, into the woods. "Are you two gonna have sex?" she heard Epstein say. "Bowchicka-wow-wow, chicka-wow-wow!"

Moonlight filtered through the branches. Tracy looked like a fairy boy, the shadows of leaves playing across his face. He took one of the Budweisers from his coat pocket, took a long sip and passed it to Mindy. She took an even longer sip, belched. Tracy lay down in the orange leaves, giving her an expectant smile. Lifting his shirt, she kissed the sunken curve of his belly, licked the navel. His stomach tensed beneath her tongue. "You like that, baby?" she asked.

"Yeah." Mindy lay across him like they did in the halls before first period. His fingers raked her back. She kissed his lips. Suddenly, Tracy shifted, gently pushed Mindy back, and a blond head filled the space hers once occupied. She stared at Tracy and Andrea as they sucked each other's tongues, making slobbery noises. Mindy continued kissing down his belly, reaching the pubic hairs peeking over his silver skull-and- crossbones belt buckle. For a moment, she considered unbuckling it. No, the kinky things could only be between them. She nestled her cheek against his denim-clad erection.

Tired from all the Devil's Night mayhem, Mindy and her friends went to eat at the truck stop where Mindy worked. They sat at a table by the rack of discount CDs by bands like Cheap Trick and Kiss, bands with more greatest hits albums than real ones. Outside, drunk teenage rednecks smoked cigarettes and danced to Ted Nugent. A kid in a camo hat ran around the lot, screaming maniacally.

"Tyler needs to go home," yelled the night manager, a pinch-faced woman. "I don't care who he's dating who works here. I don't care if he becomes some Devil's Night casualty. Get his ass out!"

"I'll tell him," sighed a plump girl at the cash register, her piercings and black lipstick clashing with her puke-green uniform. Mindy exchanged smiles with her coworker as she passed. Sylvia and Mindy were given a choice of who would work Devil's Night and who would work Halloween. Feeling the burning need to be with Tracy, Mindy took the earlier night.

Tracy watched the kids outside. "Yee-haw," he said sarcastically. Andrea sat in his lap.

"Is it hard to talk?" asked Epstein.

"Why?"

"'Cause you got that big cock in your mouth, faggot!" He threw his head back triumphantly. "Awwwwww fuuuuuck!"

"Screw you, you dirty Jew!" Tracy did his best Cartman impression. Mindy wanted to fling her Pepsi in Epstein's face.

"So, Mindy," Epstein leaned forward, "keep telling us about the fingers."

"There's six fingers," she said in a ditzy voice. "Kiss. French kiss. Handjob. Blowjob. Finger-fuck. Sex."

"You're a slut," said Epstein.

"I've only gotten to four fingers!" she said with fake indignation. "I've only gone a little. Not all the way."

"What was it like, Tracy?" Epstein asked.

"Why do you care?" asked Tracy.

"I like giving head," said Mindy. "You never get the same reaction twice." Seeing Tracy wince, she tried another tactic. "I'm so glad I'm bi. Isn't it fun, Andrea?"

"I guess," said Andrea, as if she herself hadn't made that same claim a million times. As if they hadn't made out for Tracy a million times.

"Mindy," said Epstein, "dick is much better than pussy. I'll show you mine later. You'll love it."

Tracy kissed Andrea's cheek. Mindy leaned across the table and kissed the little blond boy, with tongue. His eyes went wide. His kisses were small and polite, kind of like himself. Holding her breath, she pretended to like it when Epstein shoved his abnormally long tongue down her throat. He squeezed a boob; she didn't bother brushing his hand off.

"Aw fuck!" Epstein punched the air. He tossed a dollar on the table.

"What's that for?" she asked.

"If we give you money will you do number four on us?" The blond boy chuckled at that. "Come on. Let's contribute to the dick-sucking fund." Coins and dollars fell in front of her. "Two bucks and sixty cents. That should be enough for her."

"I don't think that's enough." Mindy still did her ditzy voice, trying not to cry.

"Is she really like this all the time?" asked Epstein.

"No," said Tracy, giving her a deadpan look. "She's faking it."

Mindy stared into her Pepsi bottle, feeling sick. "Drink it," said Epstein. "Just pretend it's cum." Tracy sighed. No rage. Not even annoyance this asshole insulted his girlfriend. Something inside Mindy withered and died.

Sylvia and Tyler kissed outside the truck stop. Cartoon jack-o'-lanterns hung over them like mistletoe. Mindy stood with Tracy, staring at the sidewalk. Holding a Budweiser with both hands, she sipped the watery beer. "Hey," she said.

"Hey."

"Do you want to just date Andrea?"

Tracy sighed, ran a hand through his hair. "I don't know. We've been getting really close lately, hanging out and shit. I mean, I like you, obviously…But, you know, to be honest, I'd rather just try the monogamy thing."

Mindy nodded. "I'd like to make things work, Tracy."

"Really? I mean, you let *Epstein* grope you!" She hung her head, feeling like a waste of life. Like a joke. Tracy gave her hand a totally platonic squeeze. "You're not mad or anything?"

"Why would I be mad?" she said, her voice cracking. "You two are my best friends. It's cool." Her love for him swelled to a flood, carrying her with it. "Tracy, I…Fuck, like…I mean…" Her clumsy tongue couldn't express what she wanted to say. "I have to go."

"Why?"

"It's almost curfew, and I gotta take the bus home. I'll be okay."

"Are you sure?"

Grinning, Mindy gave him two big thumbs up. A rusty chainsaw coated in poison ripped through her innards.

"The little Marilyn Manson kids are having a heart-to-heart!" yelled Tyler. "*The beautiful people, the beautiful people!*" This earned him a glare from Tracy. "Oh no, he's looking at me! Calm down, dude! Don't shoot the school!"

Tracy hugged Mindy. She almost let it all out on his shoulder. Almost. Biting her lip, she hurried away. Looking back, she saw Epstein say something to Tracy, jokingly. Tracy pushed him to the ground. Mindy ran past the bus stop, into the nearest McDonald's, went in a restroom stall and cried.

Mindy gave herself up to the night. And the night found her.

A black hole of loneliness filled her. Cocooned in her jacket, she walked along a muddy backroad. Stupid. Worthless. Unloved and unlovely. Any number of maniacs could be hiding in the dark woods, but she didn't care. Sipping the beer, she listened to her Korn CD, her eyes heavy with tears. "*Your throat, I take grasp/And your eyes roll back/Love racing through my veins/Your heart stops beating…*" The throat being grasped was hers. So were the eyes rolling back, the heart that stopped beating because it was broken. She blamed herself for not having a perfect body. For being a stupid little girl who fucking kissed Zack Epstein in front of him. She couldn't stop the pain, it was so deep inside her. The world grew smaller, swallowing her.

Over the trees she saw the John Roebling Bridge, a brick expanse across the Ohio that would look welcome over a castle moat. Tracy once told her a kid committed suicide off that bridge. She imagined the water filling her lungs. The veins bursting in her eyes, the world fading into blissful oblivion.

A pair of highbeams bathed her in light. Shielding her eyes with her arm, she watched a blue 1960s-type car in near perfect condition slow down beside her, a pennant that said "#14 Pete Rose" blowing from the antenna. The window rolled down. A handsome black boy with a perfectly round afro grinned at her. "You need a ride?"

*Take me anywhere*. "Hold up." The beer made her dizzy, slurred her words. "Get out the car."

"Okay." He got out. Six feet tall, dressed in bellbottom jeans and an ugly beige shirt that looked like something from a rodeo. Mindy sniffed him as he got closer.

"Are youuuuu good to drive? Because you smell like beer."

"I have been partying, but only a little. You seem like you've been partying, too."

"Shut up. I only had two beers. I need...I mean, youuuu need a sobriety test before I get in a car with youuuuu. Walk a straight line to me."

He did so.

"Okay. How many fingers am I holding up?"

"Three."

"Wrong, party boy! It's four!"

"No, actually it's three."

Mindy looked closely at her fingers. "Oh. Fuck." She giggled, embarrassed. "This sucks. I only had *two* beers." She hiccupped. "Sorry."

Taking her hand, he helped her in the car. His cold skin felt smooth like a child's. His car had an 8-track player. A pair of fuzzy dice hung from the rearview. It began to rain outside. "You want to listen to the radio?" he asked.

Mindy turned the knob from the Fifth Dimension to Foghat to the Commodores, finally landed on a Joe Cocker song she liked. The car bounced down the bumpy road, its brakes squeaking.

"Where are you from?" the boy asked.

"Covington."

"Me, too."

She hiccupped again. "Sorry. Do you go to U-Cinn or something?"

He laughed softly. He was a skinny boy, his belt cinched around his narrow waist. "I look that old? No, I'm a senior. What're you? A freshman?"

"Yeah. Do I really look that *young?*"

"Kinda. How do you like school so far?"

"It's alright. I can't wait to get out, though. I bet being a senior is soooo much cooler."

"Not really. Like, I just got accepted to Northwestern so it's like, 'Why am I even here?' Just wasting a whole year of my life in Cinci-fucking-natti."

"Northwestern?" Chicago sounded so exciting. "What're you studying?"

"International politics. I'd like to work for the UN, maybe do aid work in Africa."

"Wow. That's really cool. God, you're so lucky you're graduating!"

"So…what are you into?" he asked.

"Theatre," she said. "I don't know where I want to go to college, but I'm definitely gonna do acting. I did *Bye Bye Birdie* at school last month, and it was sooo fun."

"I thought the fall play was…" He shook his head. "Whatever. I'm glad you had fun."

Mindy felt a sad pang, remembering the roses Tracy gave her after the first performance. "It's kinda funny. Like, everybody expects me to be this mopey girl like some of my friends, and when I get onstage I'm all verbose. Well, I'm verbose offstage, too, I guess."

"I can tell."

She hiccupped. "I'm sorry. I keep hiccupping."

"That's cool. I think it's cute." Mindy's face felt warm. "So what were you up to tonight?"

"I broke up with my boyfriend."

"Oh, I'm sorry."

"Don't be. He broke up with me 'cause he wanted to be with another girl. I mean, I *did* make out with another boy in front of him. Okay, two other boys. God, I'm so stupid!"

"Everybody makes mistakes."

"That's right. And I'm cool with it. Really. Besides, being single works better for my flirtatious ways." Guys liked it when girls acted flirty. Still, Mindy hated lying. "Okay, I'm not really cool with it. Usually I don't let things get me down like this. I mean, like...I know I'm just a drunk girl and I'm probably not making any sense..."

"No, you're making a lot of sense. It hurts, but it'll all get better. And there'll be other guys. I know I only just met you, but you seem pretty cool to me."

They fell silent. She glanced at him shyly as they turned a corner. He drove expertly along the sharp curves, seeming to stare past the road. He met her eyes, glanced away. "So, um, where's your place?" he asked. "Where am I taking you?"

On his dusty dashboard, she wrote with her finger: "Mindy Alexis Snyder. July 10, 1984-Oct. 30, 1999."

"Why don't we go back to your place?" she said.

The boy started sweating.

Through the rain-blurred windshield, she saw a shopping plaza. A dollar store, a laundromat, a Michael's craft store. As the car drew closer, they all rippled like images in a disturbed pond. A new image appeared overtop of them, as if quick-drawn by some cosmic artist: a bungalow on a quiet suburban street. A porch swing, a doghouse, a single light on in a window. Parking by a curb that appeared from nowhere, the boy opened her door for her. The rain felt cool on her skin. Mist rose off the asphalt. The two teenagers didn't even make it to the front door. Smiling the cutest smile in the world, he kissed her. Mindy slid her arms under his shirt. His body felt brittle as bird bone, like she could crush him if she squeezed too hard. Brittle and cold. No matter how long she held him, he didn't get warmer. Mindy let the cold spread through her. "Let's get inside," she said. "Not out here."

"We'll have to go in through the window. Be real quiet; it's past my curfew." The boy grabbed the rusty latch, pulled on it with a grunt. It didn't budge. Gripping with both hands, he leaned back until sweat beaded his forehead. "Fuck!" Mindy took the other end and, together, they forced it up with a shrill, parent-alerting screech. The boy froze, nervous. After a minute of silence from inside, he sighed in relief.

Mindy gave him a high-five. "Go teamwork!" she said. The boy slid his gangly body through the window one leg at a time, landing awkwardly on the shag carpet. Taking her hand, he helped her in. They immediately started making out. "You're so pretty," said Mindy, caressing his sharp cheekbones. "You're so sexy."

"Shhh. My folks sleep on this floor." Carefully, she followed him past his parents' room, the door ominously ajar. Through the crack, she saw two shadowy figures snuggled in bed, in the light of a rabbit-ear TV playing *Happy Days*. Only when they reached the end of the hall did Mindy let herself breathe easy. She looked back and saw only darkness, like the hallway had been erased. Or it had never been there at all.

Indeed, it seemed the boy carried an invisible lamp, lighting the house as he passed. Everywhere they walked, she saw the rooms in clear detail: the kitchen with paisley-print wallpaper, suede furniture in the living room, sepia-tone photos hanging in the hallway. It all receded into darkness as soon as she had her back to it. He led her through a bead curtain into his basement room. He had a mattress on the floor, Sly & the Family Stone posters on the wall, a lava lamp. A vinyl record player sat atop a cassette player. Records from bands like Earth, Wind & Fire and Parliament-Funkadelic littered the carpet.

Mindy held up one of the albums, gave him a wry look. "Really? *Wings?*"

The boy shrugged. "I've always been a big Paul McCartney fan. I can't deny it; sometimes I listen to white people music."

"It's cool. I do, too. Yay, white people music!"

"You're so cute," the boy gushed with a smile. Holding her from behind, he kissed her neck. Hard, bruising kisses that made her gasp. She winced at the sting of his Arctic breath. Tilting her neck, Mindy opened her mouth and accepted his tongue.

"Are you sure you want to do this?" he asked. "I mean, are you sober? I don't want to do this if you're drunk."

"You're such a sweetie," she cooed, wrapping her arms around his slender neck. "I'm one hundred percent sober now, and I *do* want to do this." His fingers roamed over her stomach, brushing her studded belt. She sensed the anxiety in his shaking hands. "You can take my pants off, baby."

Getting on his knees, he undid her belt with some difficulty. Next came her pants, which bunched up at her knees. Together, the two of them absolutely failed to pull them down.

"Oh, God!" Mindy laughed. "This is so retarded!" Kneeling down, she pulled at them until she fell on the mattress, knocked the back of her head on the wall.

The boy rushed to her side, placed icy fingers behind her head. "Are you okay?"

"I'm sorry," she gasped in between laughs. "I'm sorry. I'm so fucking sorry." Stretching out her legs, she helped him finally pull the pants off. Mindy kissed his eyes. "You have such pretty lashes." With as much sultriness as she could muster, she said, "You can put it in, baby."

He pulled down his underwear. His dick was half-hard, a sleepy garden snake in a tangled black forest. She touched it. Immediately, she had yellow gunk webbed between her fingers. Groaning in misery, the boy put his face in his hands.

"I'm sorry," he moaned. "I suck so much."

"No, it's okay. Look." Licking her hand clean, Mindy put her lips on his dick and sucked all the way to the end. Fleshy taste. Hairs in her teeth.

"I love you," he told her afterwards.

"I love you, too," she said.

"Hold on." He opened his nightstand drawer, dug deep and, with a "Eureka!" look, pulled out a condom in a plain plastic wrapper. Mindy chuckled.

"You've probably had that since you were twelve," she said. "Try to make sure it doesn't crumble up." Hungrily, fiercely, they made out. The blood in Mindy's veins boiled. Her heart pounded fast as a speed metal drumbeat. The heat inside her body froze to ice. Moving her hands all over him, she shivered at the touch. It felt so good. The cold made her kiss him faster. The boy's breathing grew fitful. Her breath frosted. Both of them moaned with fear and longing, anticipating the moment he put it in. Locked together in a chain of exploration.

She felt numb. She felt light as mist, but Mindy only cared about the beautiful boy who would take her virginity, the way the gold crucifix around his neck caught the lamplight, the blizzard tearing through her. *You're beautiful,* a voice soothed in her mind. *You're sexy. I want you.* She wanted this. She wanted to disappear inside him. He ran his hands through her hair, started to undo the tie to let it fall free…

Mindy started as if she'd been shocked. Andrea had put the tie in her hair. Seeing Mindy's hair troubles, she'd helped her friend out. It had always been that way with them, ever since elementary school. Sharing clothes, CDs, magazines. Good times and bad times. Boys. A flood of memories came back to her, times she wouldn't trade for anything in the world. Times she didn't want to let go just yet. Breaking the kiss, Mindy looked into the boy's eyes: no longer hazel, but milky, glazed, unmoving. A set of jagged brown teeth hovered over her neck, blasting her with breath that was hot and smelled of corruption. Screaming, Mindy pushed him away.

The rush of weight back to her body struck her so hard she fell on the floor. The boy put his arm around her. "I didn't hurt you, did I?" he asked.

"I can't do it," she said, taking deep breaths to calm herself.

"That's cool," he replied, putting a blanket over her. "We don't have to do it."

"I left my friends. I should probably go call them. At home. Not that you aren't a total sweetie—"

"No, don't worry about it." He tried to sound happy, all the while holding out his arms, his hazel eyes pitiful with longing. Mindy's fear faded and she felt like hugging him. She didn't know why. Embracing his thin body, not for too long, she asked him for a ride back.

The boy drove her to the end of the backroad where he found her. She kissed him softly. "Thanks," she said. He smiled, squeezed her hand. After walking a little, Mindy looked back. The windshield obscured his face so that she only saw disembodied features floating in the dark: thick lips, broad nose, mournful eyes staring at her. Finally, the boy turned his car around and rumbled back down the road.

"Mindy!"

A pair of pickup truck headlights blinded her. Tracy jumped out, grabbed her hands. "Are you okay? We were looking all over for you!"

"Why? What happened?"

Andrea came to stand by Tracy's side. "We called your mom and she said you weren't home, so we went out looking for you. Sylvia gave us a lift."

Mindy's coworker Sylvia waved to her from the driver's seat. Her drunk boyfriend slept peacefully in the back.

"Are you okay?" Tracy asked again.

Mindy looked at Tracy and Andrea. Her best friends. "Yeah," she said, smiling. "I'm okay."

The blond boy sat in the back of the truck, moved over to make room for Mindy. Everyone she'd hung out with that night was there, except one. "What happened to Epstein?" she asked.

"Epstein was being a douche," Tracy sneered, "saying a bunch of inappropriate shit. I told him he was a fucking poser and made him go away."

"Good. Fuck Epstein. Fuck Zack Epstein up the ass with a plastic fork."

Sylvia turned the radio to a rock station. "And now, the song you've all been requesting," said the DJ. "Ever since we debuted this, it's all anybody ever asks for. This is the new Korn track, called 'Falling Away From Me,' only on W.O.X.Y., the future of rock and roll!" Mindy and Andrea hugged each other, squealing in excitement. The churning guitar blasted from the stereo. Everybody started headbanging, filling the car with flailing hair.

Hey, I'm feeling tired.
My time is gone today.
You flirt with suicide.
Sometimes, that's ok.

Sylvia pulled off the road. Spilling onto the grass, the kids danced under the full moon. Mindy, Andrea and Tracy headbanged until they felt dizzy. Mindy broke out the tango, tap dance and Irish jig. She danced with Tracy. She danced with Andrea. Tracy danced with Andrea. Laughing, the three of them collapsed in the wet leaves.

Beating me down.
Beating me, beating me
Down, down.
Into the ground.

They found Zack Epstein's body the next day. Lying in the mud along the backroads, not a mark on him. They called it a suicide. Drugs, probably. His parents suspected foul play, saying some rednecks must have killed him. For a while, Mindy's life became consumed in Important Things. Matters of Life and Death. His death struck her harder than anything ever had. She felt horrible, because she'd hated Epstein, even felt glad that he'd died. Mindy spent a year in counseling, trying to deal with the guilt.

Tracy took it the worst of anybody. His moods grew darker, his obsession with death stronger. Andrea wanted to make things work, went so far as to sleep with him, but confided to Mindy that she couldn't take his constant gloom. She dumped him, joined the pom squad sophomore year and started dating some guy on varsity. She and Mindy talked a little after that, then only waved to each other as they passed in the halls, until one day they walked by each other as strangers. To the day they graduated, Tracy called Andrea "sell-out."

Most of Mindy's friendships didn't last past high school. Some kids started liking guns and NASCAR and quickly became people she didn't want to be around. Drama, distance and disinterest killed the other friendships. She stayed friends with Tracy until college, when he sent her an email saying she was the only woman for him, how he loved her enough to take her with him to the grave. Mindy never replied.

Sometimes she went back home, visited her parents, talked to some old teachers. Inevitably, she drove down the Covington backroads; bouncing along the potholes, the branches clawing and scraping at her car. She would look out the window and see the blue Buick Skylark that crashed years ago, now a moss-covered home for rats and squirrels. When she came to the street heading back to town, she could always see the ghosts of herself, Tracy and Andrea dancing in the grass.

# HOW BROTHER ROY LOST HIS DOG, TWICE

Ole Lincoln was a good dog. A loyal companion, a good rabbit ketcher, and he never did his business inside the cabin. Y'see, that's why it hurt me so bad when he got sick. Lyin on the porch like a rug all day long, wrinkly folds o' skin spillin all round him, his brown fur gone gray. He never wanted to fetch a stick, or lick my hand. Sometimes he didn't even eat.

Fin'ly, I accepted what I had to do. Loadin my shotgun, I thought up what comfortin words I'd say to him, how I'd run my fingers through his patchy hair and tell him how much I loved him. He was there with me and Pammy after I built my cabin, just a pup in my arms. He used to roughhouse on the floor with my boys, real gentle, like he knew how kids should be treated. With a heavy heart I stepped onto the porch, expectin to see him still lyin there. But Lincoln was gone.

Into the swamp I went, where the bogs belched and a thick film covered the ponds like bad stew. I ran cross a wooden bridge where a rooster walked, head comb bobbin, feet scritch-scratchin the planks. Yellin Lincoln's name, I pushed my way through the brush. "Lincoln!" Past collapsin ole cabins that looked like grinnin skulls in the dark. Other cabins, just as rundown, with the candles o' my neighbors in the windows. "Lincoln, where is you?" Lincoln couldn't protect hisself. He couldn't run from the gators skimmin like arrows unner the misty water. All it took was one second for em to chomp down on an ole dog.

It didn't take long to find Lincoln. Lookin down in that hole, I threw my gun in the bushes and leaned against a tree to ketch my breath. It took all I had not to start cryin.

Before sunset, I buried him by the roots of a hickory. I had to shoo away five or six wild dogs who showed up. It made sense; half o' them curs was prob'ly Lincoln's kids. I put flowers on the grave, said a li'l prayer for him. Ashes to ashes, dust to dust.

"The dog musta gone chasin a rabbit," I tole my family at dinner that night. "Fell right in that hole and broke his leg. Even if that dog was still young, he couldna gotten outta that. Bled right to death." My wife, Pammy, cried when she heard that. "It ain't nothin to cry bout. That's what happens."

"Is Lincoln comin back?" one o' my daughters asked.

"No," I says, shovelin mashed potatoes in my mouth. "The dog's gone."

"Can we take a look at him?" asked one o' my sons.

"No," I says, givin him a look o' my own.

"Is Lincoln in Heben?" another son asked.

"We'll get a new dog," I says, and the matter was closed.

My cabin was bout a mile from the loggin camp. In the mornin, I hopped onto the flat bed car o' the passin log train and rode it to the camp. On the way I passed by Lincoln's grave. I couldn't even look at it.

The train took me by a stretch o' land cleared for the canal. Nothin but treestumps, tents and cabins for the ditch diggers and their families. Down to the mill I went, a great red barn spewin chimney smoke. You could hear the machinery screechin so loud it felt like a saw blade slicin your skull. Me and the other loggers waited in the sun while some man from the company stood on a hill, lookin through a telescope, workin out math on some funny instrument, readin his maps. Then he'd give orders to the foreman. After while that company man left in his Model T, and we went to cuttin trees like always.

Ankle-deep in pond water, we spent all day choppin at one big pine, our bodies pourin sweat. Half of us workin was niggers, the other half was Meskins. The sun felt hot enough to melt us. When the tree fin'ly crashed down, we chopped off the branches with our axes, hitched it to the oxen who dragged the log up the skid road. Drenched in mud, every one of us was turned brown as bark. We took every li'l moment we got to sit on the stumps and just breathe. A long day, and it wouldn't end til the foreman said so. By the end we was dog-tired. We clocked out and dragged our sore bodies to the dive to bet on the cockfights.

Us niggers walked through the front o' the colored dive, which was a gen'ral store, into the cellar, which was a bar, and got to drinkin. Then we went out back, where they stacked the milk crates in a circle. Every cock trainer claimed to have the fightinest rooster in Florida. One said he had a cock that weighed fifty pounds. Another said his rooster once took down a full-growed bulldog. After Cherokee Joe took the bets, we crowded round the circle. Smokin, swillin moonshine, watchin the fight. Them birds flew and scratched and hollered and men shouted bets and money changed hands. The fight lasted all o' half a minute, and some men argued and some came to blows and ended up huggin five minutes later. I won two dollars off the fightinest rooster, but it didn't make me no happier. I just looked at the mangled dead bird in the pit, wonderin if roosters could make good pets.

Hearin all that cheerin and singin from the boys just made my head hurt. I wandered the cypress trees by m'self, careful not to cut my hands on the sawgrass leaves. I thought o' the good times with Lincoln. Lord knows how long I walked, when I heard a familiar bark. Three rowffs in a row. "Rowff! Rowff! Rowff!"

Well, I swear it sounded just like him. Followin that rowffin, I ran til I came to a lake. A foul-smellin, mosquito-ridden place where bulrushes strangled each other for room in the wet grass. Risin from the center o' that lake like a hunchback was a small island, no bigger'n a sawdust heap. Muddy and strewn with a few rottin orange trees, the oranges black with fruit flies.

On that island I saw a red Injun. A dead one, seein as how I could see right through him. He wore knee-high boots, a pair o' leggins, a short robe sashed at the waist, two crane feathers in his long hair. A cold feelin came over me when I saw what rowffed at his feet: Lincoln, lookin and actin like he did in his prime, bouncin and scamperin noiselessly over the dirt.

"Lincoln!" I yelled, doubtin my own eyes. Squintin, I realized I could see right through Lincoln, too. His glassy black eyes was now white like a blind man's.

Now, I don't hang round ghosts, as a gen'ral rule. It's not just that they's dead, though that's part of it. It's that they don't make no plans. They never talk bout what they's doin tomorrow, cause they ain't got a tomorrow. All day and night they hang round windmills and abandoned cabins and talk bout the past. It's depressin as hell.

"Howdy," I says to the Injun. "You mind talkin a sec?" I just kept remindin m'self that talkin to a ghost wasn't too weird. Hell, I knew a fella with three shadows, and me and him got along just fine.

"If you want to talk," said the Injun, like he couldna care less, "come over here." Seein a canoe by the shore, I sat right in it and rowed to the island. It took me a while, but I made it, and climbed to the top. The hill was slippery, and I grabbed hold o' the trees for support. There used to be more of em; I heard phantom orange trees swayin in a ghostly wind. Lincoln jumped round me, sniffin at my boots and waggin his tail. I wanted to touch him, but somethin tole me that was a bad idea.

"That's a nice dog you got," says I, real friendly-like.

"I know." The Injun didn't speak no English, talkin in his gibberish tongue, but I could hear his words in the wind.

"How long's he been hangin round you?" I ask.

"Not like it's any of your business," said the Injun, "but he just wandered over here one day."

I tried to stay friendly. Ghosts is known to be grumpy sometimes. "Y'know, he used to be my dog. You ever takin him out to ketch rabbits? He's a good rabbit ketcher."

The Injun just stared at me with milky eyes. And stared. Feelin kinda spooked, I cut to it. "I'd like to have him back." Sure, he was a ghost, but he was still Lincoln. He still lay on his back and whined, waitin for someone to tickle his belly.

The Injun turned his back to me. "No."

"What use do you got for a dog?" I ask.

"What use do you have for a dead dog? If he's dead, that means he's not yours."

"The hell kinda sense do that make? That's my dog. I had him since he was a puppy. He's right there! He may be a ghost, but he's still my dog." For his part, Lincoln seemed torn, glancin between the two of us.

"I've heard enough of this." The Injun pointed to Lincoln. "Come, Osceola."

I frowned. "His name's Lincoln, not Ah-see-o-la." Osceola sounds like some sickness you get from stayin in the sun too long.

"He's named Osceola," the Injun continued, "after the great chief who led the Unconquered People against the white man." Lincoln bounded over to him, and the Injun tickled his chin. "You're brave. Just like him." He rubbed Lincoln's back. The dog's fur rippled slowly, like weeds unnerwater.

"What right do you got renamin him like that?" I ask.

"What right?" says the heathen, turnin on me. I could swear I saw a spark o' flame deep in his dead eyes. "I bet you don't even know what he is. A beagle? A terrier?"

"Course I know what he is," I says. "He's a Dog."

The Injun stuck up his chin at me. "When you Christians get married, you say 'Til death do us part.' That means, once you die, you're parted. The same goes for you and your dogs."

I was so hot I wanted to take a swing at Chief Pain-in-the-Rear, but I could see what li'l good that would do. The ghost picked up his spear.

"This is my land," he said, pokin at me with the business end, "and you'd better leave now!" The weapon looked like it wasn't made o' nothin, but I felt no need to test it out. Backin up, I slipped and tumbled down the hill, right into the water. Hurtin like holy hell, I looked up. Lincoln watched me, waggin his tail. The Injun appeared beside him. He turned and, reluctantly, Lincoln followed.

The whole train ride back, I sat on that flat bed piled high with logs, cussin bout ghosts thinkin they can do whatever they want. Then I got home and cussed all through dinner. I went to bed that night cussin. "I tell you, he's lucky," I tell my wife. "Any livin man woulda been laid flat for talkin to me like that."

"You'll work it out in the mornin, sweetheart." Pammy blew out the lamp. I couldn't sleep a wink, thinkin bout what that Injun said. "Til death do us part." I touched Pammy's wooly black curls. It had been almost twenty years since we jumped the broom, and neither of us was gettin any younger. I had a sudden image o' her on that hill, all dressed up like a squaw and walkin arm in arm with that Injun, who'd be struttin like a rooster and grinnin all big.

Jumpin outta bed, I started pacin somethin furious. Pammy watched me, concerned. "Now this mess has got to stop," I says matter-o'-factly.

“Go to bed,” she said.

“I ain’t lettin this go,” I tell her. “A man’s got to stand on principle. And Lincoln’s still my dog.”

The next day at work I was down in the dumps, tellin all the other loggers what happened durin our break. They all agreed that just cause that Injun was dead, he had no right takin other people’s dogs. They said the only reason I gave up Lincoln was cause I thought I’d lost him forever. How was I s’posed to know he’d come back?

“Ghosts is always trouble, Brothuh Roy,” this one young’un tole me. We sat on a bench in the crowded mess hall, eatin our hard bread and stew. My arms and feet felt as sore as my pride. “That one spot a coupla miles from here, there got to be so many of em carryin on that the livin folk had to move out.”

“I remember,” I says. “I was a boy when that happened.”

“And then there’s them ones by the river,” he says, “who be screamin and makin them weird faces, spookin ever’body. It’s gettin bad.”

And later in the day my foreman waddled over. This white fella with a big ole belly, like he was with child. The only time he talked to us without shoutin orders was if he thought up sum’n funny, to him at least. “Uncle Roy!” he says, grinnin big yella. “I heard about’cher pickle. Some Injun got’cher dog.”

“Yessuh,” I says.

“Good luck, Roy. You know the Injuns round here never surrendered. The US Cavalry isself couldn’t beat em, but mebbe you can.” Laughin heartily, he walked off. When he was out o’ earshot I called him a shit-brained cracker and promised to punch his teeth in first chance I got.

The longer the day drew on, the more it ate at me. I’d already failed Lincoln once. I wasn’t gonna surrender him to some snotty see-through heathen.

All that evenin, I thought bout what to do to appease the Injun and get Lincoln back. It came to me in the dead o’ night: tribute. Injuns love that ceremonial stuff. At the crack o’ dawn I took my boys rabbit huntin. I tell you, it made me miss havin ole Lincoln round. He could sniff out a rabbit from yards away, dive in a bush, grab it and shake it to death just like that. My boys, on the other hand…Now, my oldest wasn’t no shot, and my middle one kept steppin on twigs, and my youngest kept fallin asleep standin up.

Hours passed, and just as I was ready to give up my youngest wakes up long enough to yell, "Rabbit!" Swingin my rifle up, I took aim and shot that rabbit dead in the eye.

We skinned that rabbit, cooked him and served him up with corn, squash and a flask o' moonshine. Then I walked to that lake where I heard Lincoln barkin from the other side, rowed to the middle and lay the food down. Standin at the bottom o' the hill, I saw em playin fetch with a stick. The Injun took one glance at me, then went back to what he was doin. I yelled to get his attention. Nothin. I did a li'l dance like the Injuns do, singin:

Bringin you good food to eat
Ho dere, Injun; ho dere, Injun
Drinks and veggies and some meat
Ho dere, Injun; ho dere, Injun

The Injun came to the crest o' the hill.

"I can't eat!" he yelled down. "What am I supposed to do with food?" His anger made the water churn. I high-tailed it away from there.

So that didn't work. All that changed was there was a ghost rabbit unner our cabin porch for the next few days. My two daughters sat on the stoop, throwin leftover lettuce to it.

I decided to give it a few more days thought. Every day I passed by the lake. I could see that Injun sittin on a rock, whittlin an eagle out o' wood while Lincoln watched him. Playin fetch with Lincoln a bit. Beatin the dirt out his blankets, carvin hisself a pipe.

"He can't even use that pipe," I says to m'self. "What's the good in that?"

About a week passed, and ole Cherokee Joe comes up to me and claps a hand on my shoulder, smilin like we's best friends. "I heard you're havin a li'l trouble with one o' my forefathers." He had a grin like a broken saw blade.

"Yep," I says, and tole him the whole story. He smiled bigger and bigger.

"Yeah, that sounds like a chief. You niggers wouldn't unnerstand. We Cherokee are very proud. We don't like people talkin down to us. And if you make a bad first impression, well, good luck to you. That's how we is, even after we're dead."

"That so?" I says.

He smacked my shoulder. "I'll tell you what. I'm gonna help you out. I'll talk to him for you. I get a kick outta helpin folks, and I'd like to meet this ghost, anyway. Sounds like my kinda guy."

Even though we was both achin from a day o' work, we made our way to the lake. Cherokee Joe talked like he didn't know how to stop, tellin me everythin I did wrong. "You shoulda asked him his name first. We take great pride in our names. Now, I'm Joseph White Eagle. A great name. A noble name. It helps if you know the language, but you can't help that. There's no way you could know."

Cherokee Joe just kept goin on bout people and custom and linerage til we reached that lake, where we saw there wasn't no canoe no more. So, seein as it wasn't much of a lake, we waded waist-deep to the center. "I know what you're gonna say," Cherokee Joe continued. "I can say it for you. You're gonna say 'Why's all this so important?' Then I'm gonna say 'Stop bein ignorant.' You're gonna say 'I ain't bein ignorant.' And I'm gonna ignore you and keep gettin things done, cause the hardest thing in the world is explainin to ignorant folk why they're ignorant. They got no self-awareness."

I was inclined to agree.

"Now, I've dealt with ghosts before," says Cherokee Joe. "You go up to em real respectful-like. Talk to em like they're still alive. 'How you likin this weather? Oh, I don't think it's too bad. A bit rainy, but we dealt with worse. How's the kids?' Y'see, they're dead, but they don't like to *think* they're dead."

"This'un know he dead."

"Now you lissen! Where I come from round Lake Okachobee, we got ghosts all over the place. You can't walk three feet without steppin on one." We stopped before the hill. "It might be best if you don't come. The problem with you niggers is you spook too easy."

I let him go alone. Partly just to get rid o' him. Then again, he was Cherokee. Mebbe he knowed sum'n I didn't. With as much hope as I dared, I watched him clamber over the mud. Lincoln immediately started barkin.

"Good evenin," said Cherokee Joe, spreadin his arms. "How you likin this weather?" And he walked out o' my sight, speakin his native tongue.

I waited. Five minutes later, Cherokee Joe came runnin back, phantom arrows whizzin by his head.

"What happened?" I asked as he run past.

He kept hurryin through the water til we reached land. The blood drained from his face so's he looked paler'n that ghost. Once we got a good distance away, he says, "Damn spear-chuckin feather-haired throwback!"

"Huh?" I says.

"Stuck-up Seminole bastard! He says, 'Don't come talkin that Cherokee to me. This hill's Seminole land.' Damned if he don't sic his li'l dog on me. Says all we Cherokee know how to do is bend the knee. Tell your pal there ain't been Seminole up there for years. Tell him he obviously got lost. There ain't no talkin to people like that. Good luck to you. That's all I gotta say. Good luck to you."

By now, I'd just about given up hope o' seein Lincoln ever again. Later that day, I sat in my rockin chair on the porch, watchin the ghost rabbits scamper round the yard and up the trees. Soon as night started to fall, fifty of em popped up in the yard. Dead rabbits can't make no descendants, but a whole crew of ancestors had come to join the one I shot.

"You's feelin better?" Pammy asked.

"I's feelin right melancholy," I says. "But thinkin back on it, I feel like this most all the time. So it can't be too bad."

"I think you'll be fine. Just take it easy."

She set a cup of apple cider on the table beside me, started to go inside. I grabbed her hand. With a tug, I pulled her into my lap and, together, we watched the sun sink behind the cypresses.

Another day cuttin trees. It rained the night before, and we slipped and fell as we tried to chain logs in the mud. All of us was dirtier'n piglets by the time we went to the dive and gathered round the radio like kids round the storyteller. Usually we listened to them musical variety shows or cheered on the boxin matches. Jack Johnson was long gone, and with him went the glory we felt with every punch he landed, but I could still enjoy the sport.

Today the radio only talked bout news. Apparently, the stock market in New York City had crashed. Now, I don't know what a stock market is, or what it crashed into, but the gist of it was that this would make all the rich folk poor. They said white folks was throwin themselves out them big buildens rather than be poor.

"And I bet after they went splat on the ground," I says, "them New York City niggers walked up, took the shoes off their feet and kept on walkin."

I could smell whiskey breath before I even saw the man comin up behind me. "You still havin problems with that Injun, Roy?" said a likkery voice.

Duelin Dan Jones, an ole logger. He'd been a prizefighter, in his day. Now he was egg-shaped, his girth gone to fat. Duelin Dan had ghosts of his own. The shadows of his former self dragged behind him like chains, three in all. One shadow was a strong and stocky boxer; another was a father swingin his kids round; the last a devoted husband kissin his wife. He lost all his money on dogfights, and ever since then he looked like a dog, all sad and jowly. The boss let him sleep in a shack by the mill. Every time I saw him I whistled "Li'l Brown Jug."

"It's still eatin me," I says, takin a pull from my bottle, "but I reckon I'll get over it."

Duelin Dan's three shadows rose up the side o' the bar. "I's just sayin I had an idea," said Dan. "Don't mind me, though. Don't nobody lissen to an ole drunk no way."

"No," I says, "say your piece."

"Well, I was thinkin, you need to distract this ghost, right?"

"Right."

"And what do ghosts like best?"

"Spookin people."

"Exactly. So what's a good way to get him out your hair for a moment?"

I kinda saw what he was gettin at, but it didn't fit for me. "Lincoln's prob'ly stuck to that one spot," I says.

"Mebbe," said Duelin Dan, "but I don't think so. Dogs ain't attached to the past like we is. Now, why do you think this Injun's so upset?"

"He don't like niggers. Or Cherokee, for that matter. He don't seem to like nobody."

"The Seminole fought with niggers, y'know. You never heard o' Black Seminole? Escaped slaves who went into the Everglades and formed their own tribes? We fought them crackers right along with em. Lived with em and bred with em. Any problems he got has to do with him bein dead. Which, by the way, ain't the best situation to be in." He took a long pull from his flask, belched. "I's just sayin, have some sympathy. You might be a ghost, too, someday. Unless you Jesus, you ain't comin back. But never you mind me." And he trudged off, along with his shadows, to keep drinkin.

That night there was a bad storm, even worse than last time. Lightnin cracked apart the sky and my chillun cried in their bed. I let em all sleep in the bed with me and Pammy. We prayed for the storm to spare our li'l cabin, and it did. Now, I tell you this to let you know that storm shook up all the trees. On the train ride to work, I saw whole stretches of em felled by the landslide. Shredded trunks floated like toothpicks in the flooded valleys.

At work, we sawed away at a tough tree. Duelin Dan worked at it with an ax, leanin on the handle to ketch his breath. As we got halfway through, it started tiltin, groanin as it slowly, then faster, came crashin down. We tried to hold it with the chains tied round, but the earth was too loose. That tree plummeted, tearin the chain out my hands so fast it burnt my palms.

"Timber!" I yell. "Run!" We all scattered as it fell, takin other trees with it on the way down. It landed with such a crash I went flyin. Lookin up from the mud, I saw the fallen tree, leaves and debris driftin down. We got up, brushed off, asked if each other was alright. Took count o' who was there.

"Oh my God!" someone yelled from by the tree. Some o' the loggers held their hats, all solemn. Others cried. Runnin to the spot, I saw a leg stickin out from unner the tree. Every one of us was there, 'cept one. I had to put my head on another man's shoulder. Another death. I felt like my whole body was bein driven into the dirt.

"Goddamnit," said the foreman, pushin his way through us. "I gotta write this up. Now ever'body move along. Damnit! We'll spend all day draggin this tree out the mud."

Nobody moved. Dan was one of us. Crushed, like so many others.

"That ole drunk's lucky he didn't die before," said the foreman, "drinkin all that likker. Now move along!"

We all stared daggers at him, but there wasn't nothin to it. Duelin Dan had no kin, no friends. No one to mourn. He'd be just another lost soul. And, like that, I had my plan.

The next day I tole the foreman I'd been huntin round that lake and found some choice lumber. Trees so high they stabbed at the sky, so wide you had to walk an hour just to get round em. "You're a good one, Uncle Roy," he said. He gathered up two o' his bullyboys and tole me to lead him to the lumber. So's I took em in the woods, right up to the lake.

"I tell you," the boss tole his boys, as he wiped sweat off his face, "they actually expect me to write a report on that ole nigger what got crushed. Why? What're they gonna do? Send his family money?"

"You mean the drunk one?" asked his boy.

"Hell yeah! I shoulda fired him. He's more trouble dead than he was alive."

"We comin up there soon, suh," I says. "Trees as…as big as life isself."

"You sure are funny, Uncle Roy. That's what I like about you. Ain't he funny?"

"Much obliged, suh," I says.

"Sometimes I wish I could take you home," said the foreman, "tell some jokes for my friends."

"We there, suh," I says, turnin so he wouldn't see my smile.

Now, I's used to the place by now, but they was gettin creeped out around all them dead trees. "They's around the other side o' this lake," I tole em. As the foreman and his boys walked long the edge, I lagged behind a few steps. The Injun appeared, spear in hand. Like stalkin a deer, he crossed the water. No ghost can resist spookin three people. Turnin round, he waved Lincoln over.

The Injun, who was very dead, he got to the shore in no time flat. Lincoln was still new dead, so he wasn't as fast. Keepin to the bushes, I whistled for him like I used to when he was alive.

Lincoln turned his head.

"C'mere, buddy! C'mere!"

That dog was standin on top o' the water. To show I was serious, I took a few steps into the lake. I'd walk right to him if I had to. For a second, Lincoln looked at the Injun, made a low moan. Then he came lopin back to me, runnin on air, and jumped into my arms. Instead o' soft fur, I felt a cold wind blow over my bones. Ice filled my lungs.

Three voices screamed from the woods, shakin the crows out their nests, and sure enough I saw that foreman and his boys come runnin back the way they came like they'd been shot out a cannon. They went crashin through the woods and prob'ly didn't stop til they reached the sawmill. Suddenly, my whole chest went numb, my teeth chatterin. I looked down at Lincoln's head stickin out o' my breast, his long tongue hangin out his mouth.

The wind called his name. *Osceola. Osceola.* The Injun couldn't follow us, bein stuck on the lake as he was. Leadin the way, I took Lincoln far away from there.

Me and Lincoln was back together at last. We walked awhile unner the Florida sun. I started noticin things. Lincoln didn't pant in the heat because he didn't breathe. He didn't blink, neither. He didn't weigh nothin and kinda floated over the grass. I came to realize he wasn't barkin at all. He had no mouth. Sure, I felt his presence, a friendly disposition in the air, but even the sight o' him was sum'n I thought up. If I looked at him a certain way I couldn't see him at all.

Lincoln led me to an empty grove; we'd cut the trees down long ago. Sittin on a stump, I held out a tremblin hand to him. He turned to me with a breathless snort, stuck out his tongue, and my hand flinched at the touch. Lincoln lost interest, started to meander. Ants ran from him, butterflies fluttered the other way, woodpeckers stopped peckin on the treestumps. Still, Lincoln seemed right at home caperin in the trampled yellow grass, barkin at things I couldn't see. We was together again, but he wasn't with me. Not really. With that heavy-hearted feelin, I realized the Injun was right. And that felt like losin Lincoln all over again.

So's I took him back to the edge o' the water, with the apology ready on my lips. I felt sightless eyes starin down at me as I came. Sittin on the island, Chief Pain-in-the-Rear gave us a look, then turned away, whettin a spear blade that couldn't cut nothin. I realized he sharpened it cause it comforted him to do what he did when he was alive.

"You got what you wanted," he says. "Now take your dog and leave me be."

Smilin, I waved Lincoln along. "He's yours."

The Injun was suspicious. I knelt down and, even though it gave me the shivers, I passed a hand over Lincoln's fur. "Go to him, boy." Slowly, Lincoln went to the Injun, who watched as he came. The Injun smiled when Lincoln jumped in his arms, and for a moment I was jealous of that there Injun.

"What's your name?" I ask the Injun, without really thinkin. "I's sorry I never asked your name."

He thought a second. "I-I can't remember. I used to know, but now it's gone."

"Well, my name's Roy Mustang," I says, "and I guess I'll be seein y'all round." There was other things I wanted to ask, but they was the type o' things you just don't ask. So's I left the lake, whistlin to m'self.

The next day I went to see Duelin Dan, whose ghost sat on the spot where he got crushed. "How you doin?" I ask.

"I don't know," says Duelin Dan, his windy voice achin with sorrow. "I feel lonesome. Nobody talks to me." It was true; the foreman had us cuttin trees outta sight o' the new ghost. "Did you ever get your dog back?"

"Yep, but I decided it was best he stay with his own kind." A thought came to me. "Seems like I came at the right time. There's a ghost up over yonder who might use some company."

"I'd like to, but I's pretty much stuck to this spot."

Thinkin over the problem, I shoveled the dirt where Duelin Dan died and rolled it to the lake in a wheelbarrow. Seein as how he couldn't leave, he went with it. All the loggers stopped to watch as I pushed him through the trees, then the camp, the ghost hoverin over me. I was still on the clock, but nobody stopped me. They just leaned on their ax handles and watched. Some gave me a nod.

Bein his usual grumpy self, the Injun was skeptical bout the idea. But Lincoln warmed to Dan, seemed to want him around. Soon enough they was all friendly, the two men talkin while Lincoln chased butterflies.

I got a pup, named him Moses. He was a terrier. Moses jumped all over the cabin and loved playin with the kids, loved waitin by the table for food scraps. He went in the house sometimes, but I could forgive him for that.

Everythin pretty much went the way it always had. My foreman still smoked a pipe in the sawmill, amid the sawdust chokin the air and the buzzin so loud no one could think straight. Cherokee Joe still took bets on the cockfights, while the shades o' roosters watched from their warrior's rest atop the milk crates. They shone white as doves and stood tall as eagles. Ghost rabbits and all their ancestors sat in the pine branches. The dead and those who would be dead rode the train to the quarry and the sawmill. And that Injun whittled away the time with Lincoln, who he called Osceola, while the dog played ketch with the memory of a rubber ball. You could hear Duelin Dan's full-throated laughter in the babble o' the creek.

# ASSISTANT

## Chapter One
## The Death and Funeral of Richard Johnson

**Bogota, Mississippi**
**1920**

Darkness filled every corner of Elijah Creymark's single-room cabin. Elijah and his two little brothers huddled with Mama by the kettle stove. None of them dared move an inch, or breathe too loud, and they certainly wouldn't light a lantern to alert the terrors outside to their presence. Mama sang to ease their fear, a whispered hymn about going home. Pa peered out the window, his Winchester rifle at the ready. Elijah's older brothers, David and Joe, stood behind him, gripping machetes in trembling hands. For some reason he didn't know, Elijah looked out the window. Trees formed a high black wall around the cabin, and the night was thick as molasses. In the impenetrable dark, Elijah saw a child.

A little brown girl crept through the waving grass. Graceful as a firefly and just as frantic. A cold feeling clutched Elijah's gut. The girl disappeared into the woods, swallowed by the darkness. Elijah cried and cried, pressing against Mama's fat thigh. His mind stayed on the girl, praying she wouldn't be lost for long. He listened to Mama's song:

*I'm a poor pilgrim of sorrow; I'm tossed in this wide world alone*
*No hope have I for tomorrow, I started to make Heaven my home*
*Sometimes I am storm-tossed and driven*
*Sometimes I don't know where to roam*
*I heard of a place called Heaven, and I started to make it my home*

***

Manboy V. Johnson's heart exploded. Elijah knew because he was there.

Elijah and his friend Jimmy Ketchum sat on Manboy's porch like they often did, sweating in the summer sun, listening to Manboy talk to his skinny mulatto wife. The Johnsons were Elijah's closest neighbors, though they lived halfway across the valley. Their cabin always burst with people, the ever-present aroma of fried cooking colliding with the heady stench of the swamp. Manboy told stories. Great, booming, swaggering stories. He had something to say about everybody, creative insults that kept Elijah laughing for days. On the day he died, the huge man sat on a stool, fanning himself with a deck of cards and talking about Miss Edna from church.

"I got no damn idea why they made her head o' the choir," he grumbled, taking a swig from his whiskey jug. The red liquor clung to his thick black beard. Manboy had one eye. He lost the other in a knife fight, or to a stubborn pack mule, when he felt like boring Elijah with the truth. "Do you remember what happened wit' her daughter's weddin'? Do you remember, Mary?"

"There weren't no weddin'," Mrs. Johnson chuckled.

"How you gon' mess up a weddin'?" He shook his head. "That woman ain't got sense enough to pour piss out of a boot—"

Manboy suddenly clutched his chest, made a high-pitched noise like sucking air through a reed. He shot to his feet, took three steps and toppled forward. The whole porch shook from the impact. His children and grandchildren poured from the house. So many people knelt around Manboy that Elijah could barely see him. It took four sons to turn him on his back. They slapped his cheek. "Wake up, Grandpa!" "Let him get some air!" Mrs. Johnson cradled Manboy's head in her arms, crying to the sky: "Oh Lord, don't take him now!" For an instant, Elijah saw Manboy's face, his eyes staring up and open.

The pleas for Manboy to wake turned to cries of sorrow, and prayer. A grandson sang: "*One of these mornings bright and fair, I'm gonna lay down my heavy load...*" Backing away from the porch, Elijah watched Manboy's family sprawl across his still body, not knowing what to feel or if he should feel anything.

"Richard," Mrs. Johnson whimpered, caressing his cheek. "Richard, my love." That was the first time Elijah heard anyone utter Manboy's real name.

It was the first time he'd seen someone die.

The next few days were consumed with preparation for Manboy's funeral. Pa, the local carpenter, built the coffin. Mama had Elijah carry food and flower bouquets to the Johnsons' cabin. Every time, Elijah half-expected to see Manboy on the porch; his coal-black face shining in the heat, ranting about somebody. Instead he saw Mrs. Johnson sitting alone, staring out at the swamp as if in waiting. None of the grownups mentioned Manboy when Elijah came around. They chatted about how delicious the candied yams would be or how somebody needed his plow fixed, like all this was normal. Like Pa was nailing together that big box just for fun. It made Elijah angry. A month after his tenth birthday, and they still treated him like a little kid.

Elijah couldn't bring himself to feel sad about Manboy. He did, however, wonder where Manboy went. While chopping onions with Mama on the porch, the fumes stinging his eyes, he asked her, "Mama, what happen to Manboy?"

Without looking up, she answered: "He gone to Heaven."

Elijah liked thinking of Heaven, God's paradise where you got to be with your loved ones and Jesus. It scared him, too. Manboy was talking on his porch when it happened. God could take anybody at any time.

The day before Manboy's funeral, Elijah and Jimmy walked the dusty trail to Elijah's house from Mr. Jacob's general store. Pa didn't want Elijah going to the store, which stood only a mile from town. White folk lived in town. Colored folk sharecropped their land; harvesting corn, cotton, sugar cane. Elijah's butt ached just remembering the spanking he got the last time Pa found out he'd been to Mr. Jacob's. Still, he couldn't pass up the chance to buy candy. Jimmy, a light-skinned boy with reddish hair, kicked puffs of dirt off the road. Gnawing the tough candy, Elijah laughed as a chill breeze blew up his shirt. Pebbles bit into the leather-tough soles of his feet.

"You sure you don't want s'more taffy?" Jimmy asked, offering him a stick. Elijah shook his head. "Suit yourself." Jimmy chewed the stick. Elijah smiled wickedly at him and pulled a stick out of his pocket. Jimmy's eyes widened. "You stole that?"

Elijah fished in the other pocket, pulled out a small bag of tobacco. "This, too. C'mon, let's go smoke."

The ten-year-olds sat on the wooden bridge over Watchaloo Creek, legs dangling off the side. The creek snaked around the hickories, moss thick on its banks, lily pads strewn across the muddy water. Hidden animals shrieked and buzzed and croaked behind the trees. Beside Elijah, Jimmy smelled like fish. After his parents died in the Bad Day, the courts apprenticed Jimmy to an old fisherman who became his guardian. He lived with the fisherfolk on the river, catching and cleaning fish most of the day.

Elijah took a beautiful silver pipe from his pocket. It had a long, curved stem of burnished wood, and a lid on top that could open and close. "Ooh, where you get that?" Jimmy asked as Elijah packed in the tobacco.

"My Cousin Cornbread gave it to me," Elijah said proudly. "He got it from France. He was in the war, fightin' the Germans." A month ago Cornbread showed up at Elijah's door, so many medals pinned on his army uniform they clanked together when he walked. He brought treasures from far-off places: an English dagger with a painting of a knight on the handle, a Mauser pistol, photographs of the Eiffel Tower and the Riviera. French picturebooks Cornbread told Elijah he couldn't look at just yet, giving him a wink. Cornbread left for the war as just another cousin. He came back the explorer of distant lands, the man Elijah dreamed of becoming.

"Cornbread went right into Germany," said Elijah, inhaling the sweet tobacco. "And the Hun tried to take 'im down, but he shot 'em all." He pointed his finger like a pistol at Jimmy. "Bang b-b-bang bang!" Giggling, Jimmy ducked behind a tree to avoid the imaginary bullets. "Don't be scared, Jimmy!"

Jimmy jumped out, pointing his own finger-pistol. "Bang bang bang!" Elijah rolled off the bridge, landing on all fours in the creek. Scrambling to his feet, he ran under the bridge, listening for Jimmy.

Holding the pipe in one hand, finger-pistol at the ready.

"I'ma be the soldier," Elijah called up, "and you be the Hun."

"The Hun?" he heard Jimmy say. "I don't wanna be no German!"

"You a dirty, stinkin' German!" Slowly, he peered from under the bridge, looking for Jimmy in the trees. "You F.F.F., German!"

"What that mean?" Jimmy sounded close.

"Frigged, fucked up and far from home!" Cornbread taught him that one. Too late, he heard Jimmy's footsteps overhead. His friend dropped off the bridge into the creek, finger aimed right at Elijah's chest.

"Bang bang!" Jimmy gave him a stupid satisfied grin. "I got you, 'Lijah! I could see that pipe smoke so easy. You dead!"

Instead of falling down, Elijah folded his arms. "I ain't dead! And I don't wanna play no more!"

"I got you right in the chest! You dead!"

"No I ain't!" Elijah tackled him to the water. Rolling, they pummeled and kicked each other. Jimmy punched Elijah's side, but Elijah grabbed both his wrists, pushed him on his back and punched his face. Jimmy put his hands up to block the blows. "Who dead now, huh? Who dead now?"

"Elijah!" With dread, Elijah looked up to see Mama scowling on the bridge, a smudged apron around her barrel waist. Quickly, he dumped the tobacco in the creek and stuck the pipe in his pocket. He stood up, trying unsuccessfully to wipe the mud off his clothes. "Elijah, have you lost your right mind? Come home right now!"

Mama led them on the walk of shame to their cabin, the whole time grumbling about how she should make him wash the whole family's clothes by himself and how Pa should whip him with a switch. They passed the family vegetable garden, the first green tomatoes blossoming on the vine; the outhouse Pa just finished building; the small plot holding the graves of Elijah's grandparents and his uncle Cornelius. A crude wooden crucifix watched over each one. Elijah shivered at the sight of Manboy's plain pine coffin. The town wives peeled potatoes and churned butter outside the cabin. He smelled chicken sizzling on the stove, making him want to take a bite out of the air. His seven-year-old brother Thomas stopped chopping tomatoes to give him a big "you in trouble" grin.

Most of the women were Manboy's kin one way or another. If Elijah remembered right, Mama's sister had married one of his sons. Manboy's wife's mother, Miss Margaret Whittlesey, sat in a rocking chair on the porch. Wrinkly as a shriveled apple, her hair as white as ash in the fire, skin sagging off her jowls. Her lips moved in silent conversation with herself, her milky eyes half-closed.

"Sit here 'til I can get you washed," Mama ordered, gesturing to the porch with her rolling pin. The boys sat obediently on the stoop. Elijah watched Joe and David come back from the woods, carrying armfuls of firewood. Mama gave orders to the other wives, pointing the pin like a general with a sword. "Alma, boil that water. Cissy, bring me the sugar." Her face softened. "You can eat dinner here t'night, Jimmy."

"Thank you, ma'am!" said Jimmy. Elijah rolled his eyes. Miss Margaret rocked back and forth, grating on Elijah's nerves. She gently stroked a strange doll in her lap, the sight of which made him shiver. Carved from gnarled wood, it had an angry face. Bared fangs, narrowed black eyes that seemed to stare straight at him. Elijah looked away from it.

"Lizzy?" Miss Margaret asked shakily, laying sightless eyes on Elijah. He cringed. "No, y'all boys. And don't ask how I knew y'all was boys. No girls get that muddy, 'cept maybe me when I was your age. I can smell it all over you. Are you by chance the Creymark boys?"

"Yes, ma'am," said Elijah, anxious to get away from her and that doll. "Well, I am. And this here my friend Jimmy Ketchum."

"And which Creymark boy is you? Michael Earl or Michael Cornelius?"

"My name Elijah. Earl my pa." Margaret Whittlesey shook her head, making an "Mmm-mmm" sound. "What that thing in your lap?"

Miss Margaret didn't seem at all taken aback by his forwardness. Stroking the tuft of white hair atop its head, she said, "This? This was given me by a man long time ago who come live on the plantation. They brought him from the delta. Name of…of…I can't recall right now. We call him the Magic Man." Elijah sat up. Now *this* was interesting.

"Don't tell the boys things like that, Miss Margaret!" Mama said from the doorway.

A smile crossed Miss Margaret's melted wax face. "And why not? It's the truth. I always been the type o' person who tell the truth. Every fortnight, we sneak out from the quarters. Me, Ma and Pa and my sister Lizzy. We meet up at a special place in the woods, where he show us things you wouldn't believe." She whistled, like she couldn't believe it herself. "Don't think you the only one who ever done sum'n you wasn't s'posed to." She tried to laugh, but it turned into a rattling cough. Mama touched her arm. Miss Margaret waved her off.

"I'm fine. Thank you, dear. Every time we go to that clearin' we dance 'round the fire, makin' magic with our dancin'. We dance, and a storm come through and ruin all the machines. Or some beast kill all the chickens." Elijah exchanged a fearful look with Jimmy. Voodoo; dark magic.

"And the Magic Man preach to us," she continued. "Tell us we'd go back to the beginnin' when we die. Before he disappear, he tell us we'd become birds and fish, flyin' and swimmin' away from that plantation. And he give *Him* to me." She held out the tiny figure in a trembling hand. "Go 'head. Look at it."

Reluctantly, Elijah took it from her. He touched its mean, exaggerated features, careful not to get splinters. It had a scent he'd never smelled before: a sickly-sweet odor that made him think of far-off places. Elijah placed the doll back in Miss Margaret's lap, like it might burn him.

"What is it?" he asked.

"A god," she said. Elijah saw Mama throw up her hands in exasperation. "An *orisha*. The Magic Man say He'd watch over me. And He has, all this time." Miss Margaret closed her eyes, drifting to sleep. "All this time."

Five days after he died, they moved Manboy to Cemetery Hill, a clearing of overgrown grass where the trees bowed their heads in mourning. The long procession clapped and shook tambourines, singing: "*I got shoes, you got shoes, all God's children got shoes. When I get to Heaven, gonna put on my shoes and gonna walk all over God's Heaven.*" Elijah sang along, walking between his brothers: David and Joe on his right, Thomas on the left, two-year-old Simon in Mama's arms. Mama cried. Pa had his head down, silently praying. He'd thrown a terrible fit that morning because Cornbread wasn't home for the funeral, having spent another night playing guitar at the white beer halls in town.

Elijah had heard Pa complain about the job the undertaker in town did on Manboy's body, as he could tell from the faint scent of decay hanging over the casket. At one point the body shifted, forcing a pallbearer to his knees. They reached Manboy's small tombstone. The pastor read it out loud:

Richard Johnson
Born Feb. 19, 1869
Died May 5, 1920

The pastor said the last blessing. Elijah's mind wandered. He wanted to listen to Cornbread play guitar, or go fishing with his cousin. A subtle shift in the wind drew his gaze to the woods, where he saw a small boy heading into the trees. No surprise; he saw plenty of stray kids around Bogota. But why was this one at the funeral? The sound of dirt thudding on Manboy's coffin snapped Elijah from his reverie. The pallbearers shoveled it in, each clump crashing on the wood with finality.

The setting sun turned the clouds to pink scars across the sky. Elijah hauled a pail of water from Watchaloo to his cabin. Pa always had him help Mama with the cooking like he was some girl. Elijah meant to complain about this, but not today. Not with the mood Pa was in. A sputtering noise like a bad cough startled him so bad he almost dropped the pail. A cloud of dust sped up the road toward him. Elijah had heard of automobiles: motorized wagons only white folk could afford. It was a monstrous-looking thing, all black and metal and spewing smoke. His first impulse was to run, but fear turned his legs to stone. The automobile slowed down with a noise like a death-rattle. Elijah choked on its dust. Two men sat on the leather seat: a straw-haired white man holding the crank, grinning at Elijah with a mouthful of jagged brown teeth. The other sat with a slouch hat over his eyes. Elijah held his breath.

The passenger lifted his hat, revealing a handsome, freckle-faced black man. "Howdy, 'Lijah!" said Cousin Cornbread. "Shit! They makin' you do all that work?" Elijah almost fell down in relief. Cornbread sang: "*Brother 'Lijah…strollin' up that hill…Gon' carry a pail o' water…Soon he'll carry 'nother…Carryin' water 'til the sun go down…*"

Elijah made a face. "It ain't like I wanna carry the water."

The white man laughed and slapped his knee. "This your little cousin you was talkin' 'bout?" he asked in a slow, croaky voice.

"This here be Elijah Creymark, town mischief maker!" Cornbread hugged Elijah tight, squeezing a laugh out of him. His cousin seemed happy as always, though Elijah saw the dark circles under his foggy blue eyes.

The white man took off his hat and made a grand bow. "Pleased to meet'cha, Elijah," he said. He opened a trunk on the back of the automobile, pulled out a guitar and handed it to Cornbread. "You gon' play again t'night, boy?"

"Yessir, boss." Laughing, Cornbread slapped the man on the back. Elijah had never seen anybody act that way with a white man.

The man beamed down at Elijah, his whiskey breath so strong you could light it on fire. "Don't you worry 'bout your cousin, boy. Long as he play at my place, he under my protection. Other night Cornbread took me to see Ma Bee's girls. Sweetest nigger juice I ever had." He patted Elijah's head. Elijah instinctively pressed against Cornbread's leg. "Maybe ol' Cornbread'll take you someday, make a man outta you." Cornbread laughed, but not so quickly this time. The man got in his automobile, lit a corncob pipe with a match. "See you t'night, boy."

"Yes, sir!" Cornbread gave him a soldier's salute. The white man took off in his automobile, coughing and sputtering back to town. Cornbread ran a hand through Elijah's coarse hair. Pa always said Cornbread would get himself killed playing guitar in town. Elijah prayed for his cousin's safety every night before bed, and every morning Cornbread came back smiling. Cornbread started for the house, Elijah on his heels.

"Lemme carry that, 'Lijah." Cornbread plucked the bucket from Elijah's arms and held it like it weighed nothing. "They teach you to be strong in the army."

"An' I'll carry your guitar!" Elijah tried to snatch it from him, but Cornbread held it teasingly over his head. The boy thrust an accusing finger at Cornbread. "You wasn't at the funeral! You been F.F.F. all day!"

"*You* F.F.F!" Cornbread lunged at him. Elijah dodged him, ran in a circle around Cornbread until his cousin grabbed him in the crook of an arm. Cornbread hauled him in the air, swinging him around until he felt dizzy.

Cornbread let him down. "So, your Pa pretty mad at me, huh?"

"Mmm-hmm. You in trouble."

"Lemme guess, your Pa said sum'n like this," Cornbread made his voice real deep and upset, " 'I don't know what to do with that boy, Anne. I give him a place to sleep, and he ain't got the decency to go to Manboy's funeral? Jesus Christ in Heaven!' "

Elijah laughed so hard his sides hurt. "Do it again!" he said. "Talk like 'im again!"

"I tell you, 'Lijah, after while you get tired o' goin'a funerals. I know what they like. Was there women cryin'?"

"Yep. One o' Manboy's sisters was screamin' and climbin' all on the box, and they had to pull her off it."

"Did they sing 'Swing Low Sweet Chariot'?"

"Yep."

"Did they read a passage outta Psalms?"

Elijah thought a moment. "John, I think." He didn't really pay attention to that part. "Manboy stank, too!"

"Now I'm *real* glad I didn't go." Cornbread shrugged. "It ain't like ol' Manboy care whether I come. Funerals are for the livin'. The dead don't give a damn."

On the cabin porch, Pa showed Elijah's older brothers how to nail a cabinet. Elijah wanted to learn the trade, too, but Pa said he was too young. Elijah at least knew he'd do a better job than Joe. Joe couldn't even hold a hammer steady.

"How come I always gotta help Mama?" he asked Cornbread. "I wanna be wit' you. Teach me to play guitar."

Cornbread winked. "Sure, 'Lijah. *After* you help your mama. She needs a big strong man helpin' with the cookin'. By the way, you might wanna stow away that pipe I gave you before we get to the house."

Elijah stopped in his tracks. "I left it down at the creek! I'll go get it!"

"You better run," Cornbread chuckled. Elijah hurried back as fast as his legs could carry him. Knowing the woods like the beat of his own heart, he took the quickest route: around the pond where toads spawned, through the grove of rotted treestumps, under the tree where the owls slept. He reached a part of the creek where wet leaves carpeted the forest floor, lightning bugs glowed like tiny drifting stars and overhanging branches blocked all but a few strands of sunlight. His pipe sat on a stump, right where he left it. Elijah started for it, when the sound of a soft splash made him jump.

A fat little boy appeared from nowhere, creeping through the bulrushes. Dressed in muddy trousers with suspenders, the boy checked the underside of every leaf, a clump of mud in his hand. He smelled sharp and sweet like grass after the rain. Walking right by Elijah, he picked the pipe off the stump and examined it.

"Let go o' that!" Elijah yelled. The fat boy shrieked, dropped it in the creek and dove behind a tree. "That mine!"

The boy peered at him. "You left it there. How was I s'posed to know it was yours?" Younger than Elijah, he had old eyes. World-weary and wise brown eyes, like Pa's.

"You lucky I don't hit you," said Elijah, rubbing the mud off the pipe. "What'cha doin' here?"

The boy started checking leaves again. "What it look like? I'm pickin' the bugs off o' them crops, like my daddy tol' me to."

"Them ain't no crops," said Elijah. "Them's weeds."

The fat boy rolled his eyes. "Don't you got sense enough to pour piss out of a boot? I'm *practicin'*." Proudly showing his handful of grubs, the strange boy waded through the muddy creek, faster than Elijah ever saw anyone move through water. Where his feet touched the water rippled like the tiniest pebble had disturbed it. Within moments he was several yards away, darting among the trees like a leaf in autumn.

Elijah realized this was the same boy he saw leave the funeral that morning. He said that phrase Manboy always used, and the resemblance was just too strong. Maybe he was one of Manboy's thirty grandchildren.

"Hey!" he yelled, taking off after him. "Why you leave the funeral?" He felt a hundred years old instead of ten, struggling to keep up with the fleet fat boy. Elijah's eyes could barely follow him. Laughing, the boy hid from him. One moment he was skipping in the creek, the next he was behind a tree. His laughter rang from every direction. Suddenly, a deep, melodic voice boomed:

"Manboy!"

A figure stood in the creek, so tall and thin Elijah first mistook it for a tree. No, it was a man, he realized; a very old man with brown skin that stretched like parchment across his face. His three-piece suit must have looked nice once. Now it was worn; its black faded to gray, a button missing on the waistcoat, covered in muck. He wore a wide-brimmed, moth-eaten hat and a bowtie around his long neck. Thick gray hair cascaded to his shoulders. Ankledeep in the water, he regarded the fat boy, irritatedly.

"There you are," he groaned, and the hickories groaned with him.

Slowly, the old man approached, holding out his hand. The boy ran to him through a shaft of sunlight, becoming a black silhouette. Elijah had to squint to see him. The silhouette became a boy again, wrapping his arms around the old man's leg, proudly showing him the grubs. The stranger laid a boney hand on his head while looking at Elijah with eyes black as swamp water.

"Do you see him?" the man asked. His low voice reminded Elijah of a rumbling, far-off storm, and felt just as comforting. "I asked, do you see him?"

Elijah didn't understand the question, but answered anyway. "Yessir."

Holding the fat boy's hand, the stranger stepped toward him. He exuded warmth and affection; a grandfatherly aura, with a spidery sense of menace. Towering over Elijah, he looked as worn-out as his suit, like someone had folded him up and left him in a closet for a few years. His skin was withered bark, his eyes two orbs of starless night. He had a thin mouth and long piano key teeth, a beak nose too big for his face, a dagger-like gray goatee. Elijah squirmed under his gaze; the depthless eyes staring at him, into him, shrinking and swallowing him. The stranger had the pungent odor of the swamp on him, and something stronger. The sickly-sweet smell of Miss Margaret's doll, so strong Elijah felt ill, yet he didn't want to leave this man.

The stranger stared at him for a time. "Yes," he said finally, excitement in his voice. "Yes!" He grinned, wrinkles criss-crossing his face like cracks on ice. "Son, I would like to see you again. To discuss things. Could you visit me tomorrow?" Elijah nodded. He couldn't dream of saying no. "Good. I live on Berger's Hill. Look for the house that says Redbone." Taking Manboy's hand in his, he led him into the swamp. Before Elijah could ask why they didn't head for the road, they walked into the amber sunlight. He blinked and they were gone.

## Chapter Two
## The Man on Berger's Hill

"Let's say grace." Pa closed his eyes and clasped his hands. He opened one eye. "Take that off the table, Cornbread."

"Oh. Sorry." Cousin Cornbread moved the bottle of gin to his lap. Elijah laughed out loud. The family thanked the Lord and started eating their chicken, mashed potatoes and sweet, sweet buttermilk biscuits. Every time Elijah looked up from his food, Cornbread gave him a warm smile. Elijah had helped Mama cook the meal, the whole time daydreaming about the mysterious stranger.

Pa put his fork down. "Are you gonna stop playin' in town?" he asked Cornbread pointedly, not for the first time.

Cornbread waved his hand, dismissively. "Why should I?"

"There's a two-bit dive right down the road," said Pa. "You can play there, if you *have* to go to a place like that."

"Town's the only place 'round here that pays decent money."

"At the cost of your life?" Pa shot back. "What example are you settin' for the boys? I know you made some white friends in France, but that's France. Folk over here ain't like folk over there. You're a damn fool, Cornelius!" He slammed his fist on the table. Elijah pressed his back against the chair, frightened by the tense silence that followed.

"Tell us about Paris," Mama said, sounding eager to change the subject. Frowning, Pa dismembered his chicken with a knife and fork.

Cornbread washed the potatoes down with gin. "Most o' what happened there I can't say in front o' children." He gave Elijah a wink. "I loved it, though. The sights, the people, the clubs. I tell you, the Three-sixty-ninth took over Paris! Hell…" Mama glared at him sharply. "Heck, I mean. I'll tell y'all 'bout the time we met up with these English soldiers in a cabaret…"

Elijah couldn't feel the same excitement he usually felt during Cornbread's stories. The mood had been poisoned. After half an hour listening to Cornbread, Pa gruffly sent the boys to bed. He reminded Joe and David that they needed to help him with the cabinet in the morning, and Elijah felt a pang of jealousy as he knelt beside the bed and pressed his palms together. He prayed for Cornbread, for the first time afraid that God wasn't listening.

The house sweltered like an oven at night. Elijah lay at the end of the bed, under his corner of the tattered blanket. He fell asleep. In his dreams he stood in the doorway of a hut so small it could fit inside his cabin. Elijah felt like he was in someone else's body, stepping inside without thought. Five candles stood on a table. Tall and red, they blasted him with unnatural heat, calling him so strongly he could hear their siren voices. "*We can answer your questions,*" they whispered. "*But you have to come to us.*"

Elijah's eyes snapped open. The dream had seemed so real, its enticement just as strong in the waking world. Every time he tried to sleep again he saw those black eyes, smelled that sickly-sweet smell. He couldn't wait any longer. Elijah got dressed. Quietly, he climbed out the window like he did on nights he went frog hunting. Feeling a thrill of fear and excitement, he ran around the side of the house, stopped when he saw two smoke-wreathed figures on the porch. Putting his back to the wall, Elijah peeked around at them.

"Sorry if I come across as mean," Pa said, running a hand through his thinning black hair. "But, damnit, Cornbread, you remember the Bad Day! You know what happened to your pa!"

"How could I forget somethin' like that?" Cornbread passed his pipe to Pa. "I was there when they took 'im. 'We gonna barbecue this nigger!' 'Cook 'im nice and juicy!' How do I forget that shit? You act as if I don't know what crackers do to us."

"Yet you keep goin' to Satan's cesspool." Pa shook his head, drank from Cornbread's bottle. "I don't want you givin' the boys the wrong ideas. Especially 'Lijah."

"I tell 'em the good things, Earl," Cornbread sighed. "Stories to make 'em happy. I'll never forget what I saw in Germany." For a few moments, cricket chirps were the only sound. "We found a bunch o' the Hun in a trench. So our lieutenant, this white boy, he makes us charge. Forty of us went in, Earl. Five came out. A man's guts flew up and hit me in the face. I slipped and fell in a pool o' blood. They shot my friend's head clean off and his body pinned me to the dirt." His voice lowered. "They killed thirty-five of us, but they didn't kill me." Cornbread pounded his chest. "I'm a warrior. I'm a warrior. I'm a warrior…"

Icy fingers crept up Elijah's spine as Cornbread repeated the words over and over. He wanted to shout out, say something to make his cousin's sadness go away, to make him Cornbread again. Pa put an arm around Cornbread's shoulder.

"We all got our crosses to bear," said Pa. "It'll be alright."

"Yep," Cornbread said without emotion. "Can you just let me alone for a little while? I'll be okay."

Patting Cornbread on the back, Pa headed inside. Frozen in fear of being caught, Elijah let out a sigh when he heard Pa's earth-shaking snores. He waited a few minutes for Cornbread to move. Finally, Cornbread settled his six-string on his lap. Silent as a cat, Elijah headed into the tangled thicket. No one saw him go. Not even the man on the porch, strumming a lonely tune.

Berger's Hill stood halfway between Elijah's cabin and the Johnson's. It rose above the skeletal trees, a hump of red grass that narrowed to a rounded crest. The full moon seemed to balance on top of it. Although he'd kept to the road, Elijah arrived tired, reeking of the swamp and scratching a half a dozen mosquito bites. He spent the walk thinking about Cornbread. What did he do in town? Why did he act like things were okay when they weren't? The fact that his cousin was so sad made him feel sick inside. Elijah started up the weed-choked path that curved around Berger's Hill, thorns grasping at his pants. The warm night felt sticky, like bugs crawling all over him.

Manboy once told him and Jimmy how Berger's Hill got its name. Back when the French ruled what would be Mississippi, a band of runaway negro slaves joined Natchez Indian runaways in the swamp. Word spread in the French towns about the hidden negro and Natchez colony. A slave master led a two hundred-man war party to wipe it out. They called him Berger, his real name some funny French name only Manboy could pronounce. Many French died along the way, eaten by alligators, bitten by poisonous insects, strangled by noxious fumes. When they came to the gloomy hill, they were greeted not by hungry, miserable slaves ripe for capture, but a horde of fully armed Natchez and negro warriors. Like swamp demons, they fell on their oppressors with spear and sword and bloody ax, until blood permanently stained the grass. No bullet or sword could pierce their painted bodies. After the slaughter, the warriors disappeared just as quickly. Some French survivors said they faced a hundred enemies, some said a thousand. They named the hill after Berger, who had the folly to anger the spirits of the swamp.

Manboy got into the story, making "Pow! Pow!" noises for the rifles, chopping gestures for the axes, mentioning about fifty times that he had some Natchez blood. Remembering Manboy brought all Elijah's fears to the front of his mind. The night was a pitch-black beast that could swallow him whole. A hundred unseen horrors argued over how to split up his bones. He was alone in the dark, on a fool's errand, at the mercy of whatever crawled and swam and stalked the hill. He didn't know where they lurked, any more than he knew why he sought out Redbone.

Pa never told him everything about the Bad Day, but he made sure his sons knew enough. Elijah knew they descended with guns and torches, hanging and burning twelve negroes. He knew they dragged Pa's brother Cornelius behind a horse like an animal. He knew they peeled off his uncle's flesh with hot irons. He knew they took pictures of the murder and sold them as postcards. He knew there wasn't enough left of Uncle Cornelius to properly bury. Elijah passed a dead tree; gray and twisted, dotted with the shriveled remains of flowers. A humpbacked gargoyle gesturing obscenely at him with its many snake-like arms. Elijah imagined a burnt, mangled body hanging like a rag doll from its branches, the mouth open in a silent scream. The air was charred with the smell of cooked flesh. A body swung from every cypress. Elijah hurried from the phantoms, hating himself for being so scared.

Nightmarish thoughts filled his head by the time he saw the hut, an ordinary wooden shotgun house. Thatch roof, no porch, no windows. Nearby, an old skin-and-bones donkey slept tied to a rickety wagon. A lantern made from an hourglass with a candle in it hung from the roof, shedding a cone of light on the doorway plaque that Elijah couldn't read but that must have said: REDBONE. Looking at his disheveled appearance, Elijah tucked in his shirt, brushed the mud off his knees, prepared to enter when a chilling thought struck him.

Despite Pa's warnings, he and Jimmy had played on Berger's Hill before. Not once did he see a cabin.

"Come in," the silky voice drifted from inside. Elijah entered as if pulled by invisible hands. The smell of garlic choked his nostrils. He'd never seen a home so sparse. A hammock hung in a corner, one end nailed to the wall, the other to a fence post stuck in the sod floor. A blanket made of shirts and trousers sewn together lay over it. A pile of shoes filled most of the tiny room. Garlic and onion cloves hung from the ceiling. No room for company, save the spiders and roaches scuttling about. This was the home of a drifter: someone who came to town to do a job, then left for the next. The room felt hotter than outside, and had that musty scent. That Redbone scent. Mister Redbone sat on a stool, a half-circle of candles and a whiskey bottle on the table in front of him. His tie undone, coat on the floor, waistcoat unbuttoned, a cigarette in his long, delicate fingers. His eyes widened in surprise.

"Why, it's you!" he said, voice full of concern. "You should not have come here at night. You should have waited until daytime." He shrugged, lifting a shot glass in greeting. "Oh well. You're here now. I appreciate your coming."

Elijah didn't know what to say. The whole place had an uncanny feel that raised the hairs on the back of his neck. "Um, you welcome, sir."

"I apologize for the mess," Mr. Redbone said in his smooth smoker's baritone. "But as you can tell, I never stay in one place for too long. Take a seat, son." He gestured to the other stool. Elijah obliged. Mr. Redbone leaned forward, smiling. Elijah met his eyes for a moment and turned away just as quick. Hypnotic, they teased him to search for what secrets lay in their black depths. Elijah felt entranced by the room's only illumination: the five red candles from his dream. Standing in silver holders, they all burned bright save the first one, which had no flame.

Mr. Redbone downed the shot, smacking his lips. "Would you like something to eat? I could prepare some onion stew."

"No, sir."

"So polite, too." Elijah looked at the shoes on the floor. "Would you like a pair? Go ahead. Find a pair your size."

Elijah felt himself slowly losing his will to Mr. Redbone's voice. Struggling to stay alert, he searched the pile. The stranger watched him, blowing thoughtful plumes of smoke from his nostrils. Elijah never got new clothes before, just hand-me-downs, and shoes weren't included. He suddenly grew wary. Maybe the stranger was trying to tempt him with gifts. "No thank you," he said.

"You don't trust me," said the old man. It wasn't a question. "Understandable. And smart. I'll be honest about why I asked you here tonight." His eyes became slits. "How long have you seen the children?"

Elijah stammered in reply. Sweat beaded on his brow. A charismatic stranger whose very presence drew you in. The haunting, unreal aura of his home. The heat. A hundred Bible stories flashed through Elijah's mind. He put a hand on his chest, as if to stop his soul from slipping out.

"Relax." Mr. Redbone's voice was sweet water washing away his anxieties. "I assure you, I am not Lucifer."

"Who you, then?" Elijah took deep breaths, waiting for his heart to slow. "Tell me."

The old man threw his arms wide. "Just a traveling salesman for Michael's Tailored Shoes. I've traveled all over this great country, from Pittsburgh to Charlotte to Los Angeles. Now I'm in Bogota to show you these amazing products."

"That ain't what you really do," said Elijah. "If you a salesman, then how come you took that boy?"

Mr. Redbone chuckled. "Selling shoes puts money in my pocket while I travel. Very smart of you, son; I have another job." Was he a magician? One of Lucifer's minions? "I'm no one dangerous," Mr. Redbone answered his thoughts. "Now, I ask you again: How long have you seen the children?"

Elijah glanced at the floor. This man seemed able to read his mind. It frightened him, but moreso it made him want to be honest. "For a while," he said. "But only a few times." Elijah didn't know when he started seeing them. Children he'd never seen before and never saw again, even when the negroes gathered for Sunday church. He figured they were orphans, or the kids of fishermen who lived along the river. Always lost and alone, moving swift as the wind.

"Do you ever try to see them?" Mr. Redbone asked.

Elijah shook his head. "I ain't even thinkin' of 'em."

"These children…No one can see them except you and I. They are indeed lost. My job is to locate them. I have to find five in Bogota." He gestured to the candles. "I found one already."

Elijah stared closely at the snuffed-out candle. It looked lonely in the glow from the other four. Not a drop of wax had melted down the red shaft. "Manboy?" he said in disbelief. He didn't know how, but that fat little boy was the man he saw die.

"Yes."

"Where you take 'im?" Elijah asked.

"I took him home. That's my job."

"Why I see 'em?"

"You have a…talent." Mr. Redbone seemed to chew on the word a moment, deciding he liked the taste before saying it. "A gift."

"I ain't got no gifts." At least Pa didn't think so.

Mr. Redbone sighed. "You know our people come from Africa, right? You know black folk didn't start in Georgia, right?"

"Yessir." Of course Elijah knew. He wasn't stupid.

"In Africa they had people called fetish-men," Mr. Redbone

continued. "Not a very accurate term, since some of them were women. Still, a better word than 'demon-smeller,' which the white people called them. They were priests who had a second sight, who could see the things that aren't seen. Most of them were frauds; shamans who wanted power. But there were a few who truly had the gift." He stroked his goatee. "Incredible. I had lost hope of ever finding one again. Certainly not here."

Africa. Elijah had heard frightening stories of the Dark Continent. A land where cannibals feasted on human flesh in pagan ceremonies. A land of dark, ferocious beasts, and even darker magic. He got the feeling Mr. Redbone knew a lot about this place. An urge to learn more about Africa took hold of Elijah, as strong as the pull he felt from the candles.

"Your talent," continued Mr. Redbone, "this sight you have. It is something passed to you."

"You mean my parents can see 'em, too?"

Mr. Redbone steepled his fingers. "I believe the skill has slept within your family until now. Yes, now is the time for you to use it." Elijah could feel the old man's excitement, a tingling charge in the air. "What does your father do, son?"

"He a carpenter."

"I imagine he's teaching you carpentry as well?"

"Well, no," Elijah admitted grudgingly. "He teachin' my brothers."

"As he has to," said Mister Redbone. "If he doesn't pass on his skills, they will be lost. I never thought I'd meet another with the gift, not in a hundred years. Son, in you is the power of Timbuktu! The majesty of Songhai and Old Ife! To see you use this talent…I cannot pass up this opportunity. Young man, I am extending to you an offer. How would you like to help me find the children?"

"You can't get 'em yourself?"

"I'm old. It's getting hard to chase these kids around. They can't sit still; always moving, always looking. I was after Manboy for five days. Five days!" Mr. Redbone pointed his cigarette at Elijah. "You distracted him long enough for me to catch him. I could use a set of strong, young legs. I could use an assistant."

"What I gotta do?" Pa called David and Joe his "assistants."

Mr. Redbone stood up. His head almost touched the ceiling. "Talk to them, cajole them, lure them, help them feel at ease."

Elijah didn't feel at ease. "D-do you know who the next one is? I mean, can't we tell 'em?"

"I never know who it is before the flame goes out. I only get so much information." His voice became sharp steel. "Even if we did know, it would *not* be a good idea to tell them. Most people live happy lives because they have no idea when their time is. You are in a privileged position, Elijah Creymark. You can really help people. Is that something you'd like to do?"

Nobody had ever asked him that question. "I don't know much 'bout helpin' folks," he said. "I mean, I helps Mama sometime. But I'd like to help other folks! Like how white folk always killin' negroes for no reason. That ain't right at all. I could, I'd help stop that."

Mr. Redbone chuckled, thoughtfully. "As would I. With me, you'd be helping in a different way. That is, if you can handle it. It will be hard sometimes. Children can be a handful, but in the end they're so wonderful."

That moment, Mr. Redbone sounded like Mama. She told her sons she never wanted anything more in life than to be a mother, called Elijah and his brothers her "five gifts." Elijah went silent for a minute, never taking his eyes off the candles. Finally, he said, "I'ma do it."

Smiling, the old man offered Elijah his hand. It felt warm. "Remember, your apprenticeship is our secret. The business we deal in is one that scares a lot of people."

Elijah puffed out his chest. "It don't scare me."

"No. I don't believe it does. I will call on you when I need you. Until then, I look forward to us working together."

The old man's parting words lingered with Elijah on his way home. He thought of unfamiliar names, of Songhai and Old Ife. Emotions collided in him: fear, confusion, suspicion and, above all, anticipation so strong it hurt. He looked in the woods, wondering if at that very moment the lost children needed his help. Elijah climbed back through the cabin window, careful not to wake his family, and could not fall asleep no matter how he tried.

## Chapter Three
## Dark Country

Elijah didn't hear from Mr. Redbone for weeks, and started to think their meeting was a dream. In that time, he helped with Mama's chores: washing clothes, sewing, looking after his baby brother. Doing all the girl stuff while Pa, David and Joe sold furniture at the market. The stranger's face faded from his memory, until he only recalled the strange scent and the eyes like coal.

Pa and Cornbread seemed to have come to some kind of truce. Pa still complained about him going to town, but no longer did it to his face. Cornbread would be gone for days, then return in the middle of the night and sleep until the afternoon. He would offer Pa money as a means of helping out, and Pa always refused it. Cornbread would leave the cash on the kitchen table and say no more.

It got hotter. The heat was like a black dog slobbering on Elijah. Like explorers, he and Jimmy ventured into the woods, looking for hidden things. They found an ivy-covered pillar as tall as two men standing one on top the other. They found colored glass by the train track. They spent half a day digging out an old chest that was half-buried in the rock, only to find it wasn't as big as it appeared, and didn't hold any treasure. Nevertheless, Mama appreciated having a new box for her needles and thread. The boys found a grove of crabapple trees, and there Elijah decided he would build a fort with whatever spare lumber he could find. One day, three boys from down by the river showed up trying to take the apples. Elijah thought they looked like frogs, their eyes spaced far apart. A bunch of big-talking frog boys telling him they'd take what they wanted, but they didn't act so tough when Elijah came at them with a stick. Jimmy was his backup, hurling rocks. The next time they tried to steal from the sacred orchard, Elijah was ready. Wearing bandanas like the Earp Brothers, he and Jimmy ambushed them from the trees, raining down muddy rocks from Watchaloo Creek. Those frog boys beat it and never came back.

He and Tom helped Mama poke thumb-sized holes in the soil. In a season, the seeds they sowed would be tomato stalks bigger than he was. Out of all his chores, he liked planting the most. He was planting when Mr. Jessup visited. Most landowners in Bogota had inherited their stretch of wood and field. Elijah saw them out on a wagon rides, gentry in bowlers and Sunday dresses. His own landlord looked like he'd dug, clawed, and killed for his land. Mr. Jessup was a man of medium height, with gray hair in a ponytail, a shock of salt-and-pepper beard lining a jaw like a bulldog's. He could have been a pirate, in his younger days. His voice never rose above a monotone, and when he talked to Pa he stood very close.

He scared Elijah, partly because other white men feared him. According to Pa, not a single negro perished on Mr. Jessup's land during the Bad Day. When the mob came down, Mr. Jessup and his sons met them on the road. They told him to move, and he aimed his gun right at the ringleader, saying they wouldn't set foot on his property. He didn't even have to raise his voice. "That's a man you respect," Pa told his sons. "He's made of iron." Uncle Cornelius died because he didn't stay on the property. He was caught as he rode around the woods with his young son, warning every negro cabin he came to, and when the mob caught up to them he pushed the boy off the mule and into the bushes. His deeds that night seemed heroic to Elijah, but "hero" was not a word that Pa ever used.

Four weeks to the day after the meeting that might have been a dream, Margaret Whittlesey died in her sleep. The grownups said she was eighty years old. A ripe old age, they said. Longer than most, they said. The grownups started again with cooking and flower bouquets. Elijah wondered if she became a child. He couldn't imagine someone so old becoming young again.

The day after she passed, a sharecropper's wagon wheel broke by the cabin. Elijah and Jimmy played with tin soldiers they found by the train tracks, their two armies set up for an epic battle on the stoop. Mama offered a ladle of water to the sharecropper, who was busy fretting about how he'd never get his strawberries to market. "I might be able to fix it in time," Pa offered.

"I'll do it!" Cornbread declared, strolling out the cabin and yawning. He'd returned during the night, slept most of the day. Slinging the guitar over his shoulder, Cornbread scooped up a hammer and, holding it like a standard, charged the broken wagon. "Creymark!" Before Pa could say anything, Elijah, Joe, David and Thomas followed, echoing his battlecry. "Company halt!" shouted Cornbread. The boys stood soldier- straight in a line. General Cornbread paced in front of them. "Atte*nnnn*tion! Our mission is to fix this here wagon wheel." He got in David's face. "Do you have a problem with that, soldier?"

"No, sir!" said David.

Cornbread looked down at Elijah. "Do you object to this mission, soldier?"

"No, sir!" Elijah could barely stifle his giggles.

"Do you object to dancin', soldier?"

"No, sir!"

"Very good!" Cornbread climbed on the wagon and started playing a spirited tune on his guitar. Dancing a jig around the strawberry baskets, he sang:

*Ol' Jack Sprat in the berry bush*
*Met Merry Molly and made a fuss*
*Eatin' chickenberries, drinkin' cotton wine*
*For just a dime, he had a good time*
*A'fiddlin' and a'fumblin' with her dress*
*For just a dime, he had a good time*
*Havin' a good time in the bush*

Elijah scrambled on top to dance with him. Soon, the brothers and Cornbread all danced on the broken wagon. Elijah took Thomas' hands and danced in a circle with him. Jimmy watched, clapping his hands to the music. Tom jumped on Cornbread's back and hung from his neck. Elijah tried a handstand, when the scent struck him so hard he fell over. Almost obscured by the trees, the skin-and-bones donkey and wagon stood far down the road, a man in a wide-brimmed hat at the reins. Elijah hopped down, grabbed Jimmy's sleeve.

"Pa!" he yelled. "Me and Jimmy gon' go play by the creek!"

"Be back before sundown," Pa said. Mama sent him on his way

with a big wet kiss on the cheek. Elijah made a gagging face. Jimmy walked down the road with him until they were out of sight of the cabin.

"You wanna play soldiers?" he asked excitedly, shaking the bag of tin men.

Elijah gripped his shoulders, looked him in the eyes. "We ain't really gon' play now. I gotta go do sum'n. But if my mama ever ask, tell her I was playin' wit' you."

"What'cha doin'?"

"I gots me a job," he pointed at the silhouetted wagon, "with that fella. Please back me up if Mama ask. C'mon, can you do that for me?"

Jimmy frowned. "I guess. What job you doin'? Can I come?" For a second Elijah thought of inviting him. No, it was his and Mister Redbone's secret, though it took all he had to keep from crowing it to the sky. *I'm an assistant.*

"Nah," he said. "Go and play wit' somebody else." He'd never seen Jimmy play with anyone else, but he didn't want to think about that now. Elijah ran to Mr. Redbone, leaving Jimmy to shuffle aimlessly down the road.

Mr. Redbone tipped his hat. "I trust that you're ready."

Smiling, Elijah nodded. The wood on the cart had aged to a dull gray. The shoes piled in the back smelled sinfully bad. Elijah noticed some writing on the side. He'd learned a little reading in his one year of school. "M-mek…"

Mr. Redbone traced a finger over the letters. "Michael's Tailored Shoes. Established First, June, Eighteen Sixty-five. The best from Chicago." Elijah pouted. He didn't want to sell shoes. "I trust you heard the news about Miss Margaret? The entire town weeps for her."

"She seemed nice," Elijah said, shrugging. "I ain't know'd her too well."

"Well, you can do this one last thing for her." He extended a hand, helped Elijah onto the wagon. They set off down the bumpy road, the wagon wobbling like it could fall apart any second.

"Where you take 'em?" Elijah asked.

"Take who?"

"The chillun. Where they go?"

Mr. Redbone dumped an armful of shoes in his lap. "Here. Polish these." Grumbling, Elijah began polishing. "What do you know about Margaret Whittlesey?"

Elijah thought a minute. "Um, she was real old. And she was Manboy's wife's mama. She wasn't at his funeral, though." Too busy dying, he realized. "I ain't seen her a lot, 'cept at church. She seemed real nice, but she told these real scary stories 'bout voodoo magic. Oh, and she had this real creepy doll she carry 'round."

Mr. Redbone chuckled, like he recalled a private joke. "Where did she grow up?"

"On one o' the ol' plantations 'round here."

"Good job." Elijah didn't know what for. "Now polish those shoes."

The day went horribly uneventful. Journeying down the dirt road, Mr. Redbone hummed a tuneless song. He called the donkey Denny, giving her playful slaps on the rump. Miserable from the shoe stench, Elijah sweated in the merciless sun. They crested the valley and saw the neverending treetops spread out like clouds. White Heaven above and green Heaven below. Elijah pointed out to Mr. Redbone the clearing where the negroes had revival. Negro sharecroppers in straw hats went about their daily routine, watering the cotton and picking the leaves. In the distance, cornfields stretched like a golden sea.

They met precious few people on the road. Mr. Redbone tipped his hat to the occasional farmer on his way to market. It occurred to Elijah that the old man seemed in no real hurry to sell any shoes. Yawning, he tried to think happy thoughts. If he thought bad things, Mr. Redbone would probably know and get insulted. He thought about dancing on the wagon and singing about Jack Sprat and Merry Molly. That made him laugh. After what seemed like years, Mr. Redbone reined the donkey by a two-room shack. A skinny guitar man and a too-wide woman drank gin on the porch. A moody harmonica song drifted from the door; mysterious, dangerous, luring Elijah with a taste of sin.

"Go sell," said Mr. Redbone, handing Elijah a pair of beat-up shoes. "They're ten dollars a pair."

"Ten dollar? Ain't nobody got that kinda money!"

"Just do it!"

Elijah approached the couple, peering inside the shack as he did so. Six girls went about kitchen chores. *They have a lot of daughters,* Elijah thought. A shirtless harmonica player took a daughter into the other room. Suddenly, the side-whiskered man blocked Elijah's view, smiling lopsided at him.

"Well, who be this young man?" he asked.

"Elijah Creymark, sir."

"Earl's boy!" he exclaimed, sliding a beer bottle along the neck of his guitar. It made a sound like a cat in heat. "You an apprentice now?" Stroking his whiskers, he looked at Mr. Redbone. "Howdy, suh! I heard this'un like to play 'round all the time. You best watch out fuh him, suh."

*Earl's boy*. Swallowing his pride, Elijah said, "Would you like to buy some shoes? They, uh, they from Chicago. The best. Uh, Michael's Shoes…"

"You sellin' shoes?" The woman let out a great whooping laugh. "Goddamn, son, that old man workin' you to death. My girls do need a new pair, though. How much they cost?"

"Ten dollar," Elijah mumbled. He couldn't even look her in the eyes.

The woman laughed again. "Shit, son! Ain't no nigger got that kinda money! Y'all best lower that price, unless y'all figger on sellin' to white folk!" She laughed uproariously at her own joke. Defeated, Elijah trudged back to the wagon.

"Hey, when's Cornbread gonna come play wit' me again?" the guitar man yelled after him. "Tell your cousin to get his ass on down to Ma Bee's. Tell 'im Leadbelly was askin' for 'im."

"Tell 'im yourself," Elijah muttered as he climbed on the wagon. "'Earl's boy.' My name's *Elijah*." He felt Mr. Redbone's gaze on him. "Why you make me do that?"

"Our purpose is to guide," the old man stated, "to draw people to us. If you can't talk to people, how do you expect to deal with the children?" Redbone lashed the donkey into movement. Groaning, Elijah kicked the footrest. *Bump bump bump*.

"Stop doing that," said Mr. Redbone.

"Stop doin' what?" *Bump*. "Tell me where you take the chillun an' I'll stop." *Bump. Bump.*

Mr. Redbone grabbed his leg. "Why don't I give you some training?"

"Why? I couldn't even sell them shoes." He felt so useless.

"The first thing is to stop selling yourself short. You are not some ordinary boy who helps with his mother's chores. You are a gifted young man upholding a long tradition. You are a specialist, and I will not hear otherwise."

*Specialist*. The word sounded nice. "What I gotta do?"

"Close your eyes." Elijah did so. "Now think about the child. Try to picture her." Birds chirped around him. The sway of the wagon dizzied him. Elijah thought of Mr. Redbone and his scent, the home he spoke of. He pictured Manboy running along Watchaloo Creek. He pictured the second candle, blood-red on Mr. Redbone's table. "There!" Redbone's voice slipped into his thoughts. "There you have it!" Elijah focused on that candle, until he smelled its bittersweet scent, felt the warmth from it though its flame had died. "Yes! Very good, Elijah!" A fresh scent hit his nostrils, the hard work smell of dirt and sweat, bringing an image of a girl scampering through the cornfields. Lost, but definitely not afraid. He opened his eyes and pointed at the fields, barely able to contain his excitement.

"She down that way!" A flock of crows swooped over the field, coming to rest on a scarecrow's patchwork shoulders. Elijah saw the girl's head peek over the stalks.

"Very good," said Mr. Redbone. "And in no time, too." Elijah smiled at that. "Now go get her."

"Huh? Why I gotta do that?"

"Boy, I employed you for your strong legs, not your tongue. Now go!" Mister Redbone shooed him off the wagon. Elijah felt silly, retrieving some dumb girl from a field. At least he could get away from that awful shoe smell.

"And be quick about it, now!" Mr. Redbone called as he headed into the corn. Elijah thought of several replies, but didn't say them. The stalks grew high and close. He could barely see around them as he parted them, let alone find the girl. Her scent danced and roved and scurried around the corn jungle. Just as Elijah began to lose hope, something sprang out, pinning him hard to the ground. He stared up into the grinning face of a girl around his age. She wore a drab gray smock, her hair pulled back in a thick brown braid. Her hazel eyes slanted at the ends like the corners of a smile.

"Get off o' me!" Elijah yelled. He squirmed beneath her, but she had the strength of three grown men. Laughing, she rolled off him.

"Haw haw haw! You shoulda seen the look on your face!"

"You got a real terrible laugh," Elijah said, climbing to his feet. "C'mon. I gotta take you to Mister Redbone."

She scrunched up her face. "Why? Who he? I'm lookin' for Lizzy. Ha' you seen her?"

Elijah rolled his eyes. "No, I ain't seen her. But we gotta get goin'."

"Me and Lizzy gonna go see the Magic Man!" She jumped up and down.

"Girls is so weird," said Elijah.

"*You* weird! And you stink! C'mon, we so close!" Grabbing his right hand in a crushing, ice-cold grip, she sped through the corn like sunlight speeds over clear water. The stalks parted for her, whistling a happy tune. Carried by the wind, she half-pulled, half-dragged him deeper and deeper into the corn. They burst onto a long stretch of farmland dotted with fields and cabins. Elijah saw men dragging plows behind their horses. A plantation house loomed in the distance. The girl looked around, frantic.

"Where the quarters?" she cried. "Where Ma and Pa? Where Lizzy?" She looked at him pleadingly. "Where *is* they?"

She released him, and Elijah rubbed feeling back into his numb hand. The girl pointed to a nearby cabin. "They gotta be over there!" Before he could catch her, she ran straight for the house.

"Come back here, girl!" Elijah yelled, following her. He heard the panic in his own voice, realizing where they were. Cold dread prickled his skin.

"My name Maggie!" she declared. The sun washed over her, making her glow yellow-red. Elijah groped blindly at her shimmering image. His hand closed on solid flesh.

“Maggie!” he said. Giving him an angry glare, she wrenched her arm away so hard he almost fell over. “Look, Maggie. This white folk land, and if they find us sum’n bad’s gon’ happen!” He looked around, expecting to see a white man any moment. “Black folk ain’t lived here for years! C’mon!” Elijah tugged her arm. Maggie slapped him on the forehead.

“Don’t get rough,” she said. “Haw haw haw! You funny!” More annoyed than ever, Elijah prepared to retort when he saw something that almost stopped his heart.

A white boy in dirty overalls watched them from the cabin door.

“You ain’t s’posed to be here!” he yelled, pointing a pitchfork at Elijah. He looked back. “Pa, there a little nigger boy out here talkin’ to hisself!”

Elijah ran like Satan himself had appeared. Behind him, he heard the click-clack of boots on the porch, and a gruff voice. “Where he at?” Elijah ducked under a clothesline, dirty shirts clinging to his face. The chickens in the coop squawked and flapped their wings. Elijah dropped behind a well. Crouching against the brick, he breathed shallowly. Maggie skipped over to him, sat down Indian style.

“Why you run off like that?” she asked. Part of him wanted to just leave this stupid girl. Instead, he held her hand tight. His heart beat so loud he feared the farmer could hear it. “Who comin’?”

“The white man comin’,” Elijah whispered, listening for the sharecropper. He didn’t know why he told her. The look on her face told him she didn’t care.

Maggie made a defiant face. “I ain’t afraid o’ them. The Magic Man’ll help us. Other day he gave me a charm, and me and Lizzy put it in the chicken feed. All the chickens started layin’ bad eggs.”

“Come on out, boy!” came the farmer’s voice. “I got a gun! What you steal?”

“Dear God,” Elijah whispered. “Please don’t let ‘em catch me. I’ma be good from now on, I swear.”

“You really afraid,” Maggie said in disgust. “Boys always wanna act so tough, then they get scared over nothin’. Jus’ like I always said.”

“Shut up!” he hissed. “If they catch us…” Images of the Bad Day flashed in his mind, mangled bodies and carrion crows. Suddenly, a hand grabbed his shirt and yanked him to his feet. The white boy's angry face stared right into his. He had fiery red cheeks and eyes like rusty dimes.

"I got him, Pa—" Elijah kicked without thought, his foot connecting with the white boy's stomach. The boy doubled over, dropping him. Running on pure instinct, the need to live another day, he dashed into the cornfield.

"Boy!" The farmer's voice only made him run faster. Elijah fell on his knees and crawled along the cold, wet dirt, right into the scarecrow. Cawing angrily, the crows took to the air. Surrounded by towering stalks, he curled into a ball, making himself as small as possible. The blinding sun peeked indifferently through the husks. This was it. He was going to die. Hot tears ran down his cheeks.

"You hurtin' me." The voice next to him startled Elijah. In his panic, he forgot he'd been gripping Maggie's hand. He let go.

"You shoulda talked to 'em," she continued in that stupid know-it-all voice. He wished he'd left her. "Maybe they was gon' take me home."

"You'll never see your damn home!" Elijah said. "Ma and Pa and Lizzy all dead and you'll never see 'em again!"

For a moment she looked angry. Then she put her face in her hands. He couldn't believe it. The damn girl was crying!

"Where is they?" she cried. "I done looked for 'em for so long! They lef' me!" Her sadness fell over them like a shroud, shutting out the sunlight. Elijah wanted to go home. All he had to do was get to the road and head back the way he came. Everything would be waiting for him: Watchaloo Creek, the cabin. Pa, Mama, Cornbread, David always trying to act grownup, Joe, Tom, Simon just learning to walk. He could always find them. Hearing Maggie's sniffles, Elijah looked at her with newfound pity. His fears seemed small and petty next to hers. A thought suddenly occurred to him.

"Look, Mister Redbone can take you where you wanna go! I don't know where it is, but this place ain't your home no more!"

She looked up at him. "Where he takin' me?"

Where? Elijah had wondered that himself. An idea bloomed in his head, growing larger and more beautiful as the flower grows. A place he'd never seen, yet more familiar than his cabin. A true home with wonders he couldn't imagine. The thought of it gave him a warm feeling that burned away his fear, leaving only resolve.

"Do you remember them meetin's you and Lizzy go to?"

"Yes'm."

"Do you remember what the Magic Man told you 'bout goin' back to the beginnin'?" He gripped her shoulders, unable to hide his excitement. "That's where Mister Redbone gon' take you. And you can see Ma and Pa and Lizzy an' ever'body!"

"Really?" Tears glistened in her eyes. Elijah nodded.

"But we gotta go now!" he said. "Mister Redbone don't like to wait."

"Where you at, boy?" the farmer shouted from mere feet away. Before Elijah could scream in fright, a song spread over the field like water. A lullaby, in a voice deep and beautiful as a choir of angels, piercing into Elijah's soul:

*Go East on a sun-kissed morning*
*Go past all you wish to leave behind*
*Go East, like the bird be soaring*
*My son, my child, loved one of mine*
*Go thou to where the sun does keep*
*Go now to lay thy head*
*Go blow out the light before you sleep*
*My dear, my daughter, believe all I have said*

Crying from the beauty of it, Elijah felt a presence so powerful it staggered his mind, making him want to get on his knees in worship. The feeling passed, and he saw Mr. Redbone standing over him. Taller, more natural than the cornstalks. Maggie's sadness had ceased, and the sun summoned enough courage to come out again. He heard the sharecropper stagger through the corn, away from them. Maggie hugged the old man. Gathering them in his arms like a mother raven, Redbone ushered them back to the wagon. Elijah thought of where Maggie would go and envied her. He wanted to see it, more than anything in the world.

## Chapter Four
## Another Man's Coat

For the next three weeks, Elijah looked for children everywhere. He kept an eye out while gardening the family's little plot, or getting water from Watchaloo Creek. He scoured the woods, checking every branch for a child's smile, listening for feather-soft footsteps. And he smelled Redbone's scent everywhere. It teased him along the creek. It wafted thin as smoke around the train tracks. It hollered and roared around Berger's Hill.

He visited Mr. Redbone every other day. Jimmy had no problem covering for him, though Elijah still wouldn't tell him where he went. No need to ruin the secret. Elijah earned a quarter off every pair of shoes they sold. Admittedly, it wasn't much, but he saved almost two dollars in a jar he put under the stoop. Mostly, Redbone made him polish shoes and work on his pitch.

"Michael's Tailored Shoes!" Elijah would say. "Wore by the Rockefellers and the Crowned Heads of Europe! You can't live without 'em!" Mr. Redbone would cook onion soup and send him on his way at sunset. Every time, Elijah paid close attention to the next candle, watching the flame dim.

On the third visit, Mr. Redbone caught Elijah staring hard into a paperback book lying on the table. "Oh!" said the man. "Would you like to learn some reading?"

"No." Just looking at all the symbols smooshed together made his eyes hurt. He closed the book. "What use do I got for readin'?"

Redbone looked disappointed. "Well, if you're a salesman, knowing a few words gives you an advantage over someone who doesn't know any."

Elijah didn't want to learn how to trick people. "I wants to know sum'n I can use," he said. "Like, how come we only use gum to fix the shoes? Ain't you s'posed to use nails?"

Giving a curt nod, Redbone picked up a shoe from the pile. Its sole flapped loose like a big brown tongue. “Watch closely,” he said, picking a hammer and nails off the floor, sitting down at the table. Smiling, the boy stood on his tiptoes to get a good look.

On his fifth visit he told Mr. Redbone how he looked for children, getting a stern look from the old man.

“You won’t see another one until the next candle,” Mr. Redbone said, lighting a cookfire with matches. In the day, Berger’s Hill didn’t seem so scary. The gibbering night demons became squirrels and foxes. The dead tree looked more sad than frightening. Denny chomped on red grass.

“You sure you ain’t know who it be?” Elijah asked.

“I have my suspicions,” said Mr. Redbone. “When you see the next child, try to act calmly. I’m still upset with the way you handled Maggie.” Elijah rolled his eyes. He’d heard this enough times. “You put yourself in a very dangerous situation, following her around that farm. From what you told me, you didn’t do anything but insult her. You need to be soothing, convincing. You don’t want to repeat what happened.” That was true; Elijah had nightmares about being endlessly chased around the plantation.

“We were lucky, in a way,” the old man admitted. “The children always go to a place they felt at home. Of course, it is not their home, and they keep looking.” He smiled. “If that little spitfire had grown tired of the plantation, we wouldn’t have found her in a hundred years. Are you listening?”

“Yep,” laughed Elijah, rolling down the hill. He got up, covered in grass. He remembered Maggie’s excitement as Mr. Redbone took her in his cart, rambling off questions until the sun kissed them from sight. “What happen to that white man?”

“He’s going east,” said Mr. Redbone. “For a very long time.” His tone made it clear he regretted using that power. Mr. Redbone handed him a bucket. “Get some water for the stew.”

Racing to a tiny stream, Elijah scooped water in the bucket, tossed it in the air and dodged to the side before it hit him. He did this several times, giggling as it splashed cold around his bare feet. "You said the chillun get lost?"

"Yes."

Elijah grinned. "What you mean is, they F.F.F.?"

Mister Redbone frowned. "I wouldn't put it so crudely, but yes, they are." As Elijah prepared to toss the water again, claw-like fingers grabbed his wrist. "I asked for an assistant. What I got was a grasshopper."

"Oh, alright." Elijah filled the bucket and returned with him to the cabin, giving Denny a scratch behind her ears. The donkey whinnied in satisfaction. In the daylight, Mr. Redbone's hut looked like a strong breath could knock it down. "When the next candle gon' go out?"

Mr. Redbone led him inside. The third candle flickered weakly. "Soon. I have spent the day listening for clues as to who it might be."

Elijah touched the candle's cold wax, trying to think of who might die soon. A bunch of people at church were old. Manboy's wife looked older every day since her husband died. The thought of Mrs. Johnson dying made him tear up a little. "Do we have to let 'em die?" he asked, wiping his eyes. "Can't we just relight the candle or sum'n?"

"Relight the candle," Mr. Redbone repeated softly. "Or something. We can." Elijah's heart sang with hope. *We can.* "But we won't. We are merely the guides." His icy glare told Elijah the conversation was over. The boy remembered the white sharecropper walking forever east, and at that moment feared his mentor.

Returning home, Elijah saw Pa and Cornbread in the yard; Pa on top the hill, Cornbread at the bottom. His cousin held a headless chicken by the feet, a kettle of boiling water in the other hand. Cheeks puffed with tobacco, Cornbread strung the carcass up on a wooden rack, poured the water on it. No matter how many times he smelled it, Elijah never got used to the stench of wet, scalding flesh. He turned his head to keep from retching.

"Evenin', 'Lijah." Cornbread rumpled his hair, but that was it.

"How's that comin' 'long, Cornbread?" Pa asked.

"Looks like it's comin' fine," said Cornbread, plucking the wet feathers. "You sent me to buy a chicken. I bought it. Matter o' fact, I'm pluckin'it right now."

"I remember askin' you to buy two chickens."

"That ol' nigger you sent me to is disagreeable. I ain't felt like givin' that fat piece o' jelly more money than I had to." Elijah couldn't get used to their arguing, either. Caught in the middle, it made him feel like big stones were pressing on his head from either side.

"We been buyin' chickens from 'im for years…"

"You know he beats his wife?"

Elijah watched Pa clench and unclench his jaw. "Ever'body know that, Cornbread," Pa said flatly. "What that got to do wit' anythin'?"

Cornbread spit a black gob on the grass. "She was pretty, before her face got all swoll' up. I don't understand men who beat on pretty women. You wanna beat somebody, beat an ugly woman." He glanced at Pa, then at Elijah, and sighed, like the boy's presence was one more thing he had to deal with.

"I'm guessin' you ain't even try to get past your problems wit' 'im," Pa said.

"Earl, how would you know what I did or did not do?"

"I know it's pretty damn hard to feed eight people wit' one chicken."

Cornbread yanked off a handful of feathers. Seeing the stormclouds gather on his cousin's face, Elijah thought it best to head inside. To his surprise, Pa waved him over.

His father was working on a chair, nailing the legs into the seat. "Can you bring me that lumber?" Pa asked, nodding to a heap of thin boards. Gathering them in his arms, Elijah carried the heavy wood, dumped them in front of Pa.

"Hold this leg," said Pa. He took the boy's hand, put it firmly around the leg. "Hold it tight." Elijah held it so hard his knuckles whitened. With two strong blows, Pa drove the nail in. The leg was attached, stable under the seat.

Pa propped a larger piece of lumber on top a rock, so one end of it stuck in the air. He picked a handsaw out of the grass. Elijah saw the small scars on his pa's hands, the marks of his trade. "Put your weight on this," said Pa. Elijah put his hands and knees on the board, which sagged a bit under his weight. He watched in interest as Pa measured the length he wanted with his hand. Making a tiny cut at the two-and-a-half hands mark, he began sawing. The wood rocked beneath Elijah, so he pressed harder on it. Back and forth Pa moved the rusty blade, showering sawdust on the grass, on his arms. The saw caught halfway through, so he sawed on the other side, until the piece fell with a clatter. Elijah marveled at the cleanness of the cut.

Taking a rag out his pocket, Pa wiped his forehead. "Can you bring me that large piece over there?" he asked, pointing to a long piece of thick lumber.

Elijah tried, but it weighed a ton. Straining all he could, the boy barely got it off the ground. "I'm sorry, Pa," he said. "I'll try again."

"You can't lift it now," said Pa. "One day, you will. Then, you can help me with the carpentry. You just ain't got the strength right now." He put a big, scarred hand on Elijah's shoulder. "Til then, there are other ways you can help. You understand?"

"Yessir," said Elijah, getting Pa's point.

"And I guess now you gon' explain some things to me," said Pa, brow furrowing. "Like why Misses Clanghorn came over here carryin' on 'bout how you sold her a pair of shoes. What have you been doin'? Who this Mister Redbone?"

Elijah's gut clenched. "Well…"

"Don't lie to me, boy. I can tell when you lie."

"He just a salesman. He stayin' round for 'while. All I do is polish shoes and help 'im sell, and he pay me."

Pa's eyes narrowed. "How much?"

"Twenty-five cent off every shoe. And I can fix shoes!" He pointed to Pa's feet, his falling-apart workboots. "I could nail them back together no problem."

Pa stood quiet a moment, rubbing his scruffy chin. "Cobblin', huh? Well, I was workin' a job when I was your age. You should have told me. I want to meet this Mister Redbone. Tell 'im to come over, and I'll say whether you can keep this job."

"Good mornin', sir!" said Elijah.

"Good morning," said Mr. Redbone, walking away from him. The skies were gray over Berger's Hill, the clouds full with rain.

"Can I have just a moment of your time?" Elijah followed at his side. "I wanna talk to you 'bout these wonderful shoes. No offense, but you do look in line for a new pair."

"Thank you, son, but I'm in a hurry."

"It'll just take a minute. Take a look at this pair." He held them up for Mr. Redbone to see. "Real leather. My feet was a mess. I had so many blisters I could barely walk. Ever since I tried these shoes, I been dancin'." And he did a little soft-shoe, just to show him.

Mr. Redbone pursed his thin lips. Taking the shoes from Elijah, he slid his fingers over the heel, the sole. "They do feel nice. How much are they?"

"Five dollars."

"No thank you." He resumed walking.

"But, sir..."

Redbone stopped in his tracks, spun around, and Elijah knew he'd messed up again. "There's how you fail," said Mr. Redbone. "You sound desperate. Always sound confident in your product, no matter what they say. Good job on the cute kid act, though."

Elijah folded his arms. "I sold a pair yesterday."

"You let them haggle down the price. I hardly call that good salesmanship."

It seemed so stupid. Nobody could buy five dollar shoes. "I don't wanna practice my pitch no more," Elijah said, and sat right down, to show that he would not be moved. He'd worked on the dumb pitch, and polished every shoe at least twice, until he ran out of polish and used his own spit. What he wanted to do was tell Mr. Redbone what Pa had said, but felt afraid to do so. "Ain't you gone all over the place? Tell me 'bout the Sahara."

"It's hot," said Mr. Redbone.

"Have you gone to Africa?"

"Yes," said Mr. Redbone. "The Sahara is actually in Africa."

"Have you gone to…uh…Germany?"

Mr. Redbone smiled. "You want to know about Germany? Alright. Germany, or Deutschland, as the Germans call it, is beautiful. It's all lush green mountains. There are forests, with castles."

"Wit' kings in 'em?" Elijah leaned forward so he wouldn't miss a word.

"No kings. And a lot of those forests are gone, thanks to the war. There are black people there, whose ancestors came over when Germany conquered their lands."

"*Black* Germans? Do that mean they like colored folk over there?"

He always figured Germans must be mean, to fight Cornbread like they did. But maybe Germany had some white folks like the ones in France.

Mr. Redbone seemed to think a moment before he spoke. "There are mean-hearted people everywhere. And good ones, of course. Including in Germany."

Elijah looked at the grass. Cornbread told him he took a long trip on a boat to get to Europe. That it was a world away. Times like this he felt like there was a fence around Bogota, and he could never cross it.

"So," said Mr. Redbone, "your pa wants to meet with me?"

"Huh?" Elijah could have kicked himself. Of course Redbone would find out. "I'm sorry. I shoulda told you. He just wanna know who you are, and I tol' 'im you was just a salesman, and…"

"Quiet." Mr. Redbone said the word softly, but firmly. "That's it for today; it's going to rain. Tell your pa that I'll come for dinner tomorrow night. You had better wash up, too, since you'll be having company."

Silently, the rain season came to Bogota, a steady downpour that lasted nearly all day. The Mississippi delta, reminding them it was still there beyond the trees, still powerful. Rain lashed at Elijah's cabin, leaving yellow streaks on the wood, turning the road into a quagmire of churned-up mud. In the twilight after the storm, the boy stood in the doorway, biting his lip as he looked for sight of the donkey and wagon. Inside, Cornbread was tuning his guitar, ready to leave. This time Pa didn't complain, sitting at the dinner table like he was, calmly awaiting Mr. Redbone.

Cornbread's leaving instantly made Elijah more nervous. Pa was his usual gruff self, Mama obsessed with getting the house ready for company; Tom acted jealous and his older brothers didn't care. Only Cornbread congratulated him on getting a job.

"Your face ain't clean," Mama said to Tom. "Go wash it again!"

"But it's 'Lijah's boss," Tom whined, "not mine! And when do I get to have a job?"

"Boy, if you don't wash your face…"

While thinking about how useless his brother could be, Elijah noticed Mr. Redbone and Denny coming. He wore a different suit, if not exactly a brand-new one. A brown coat, gold paint flaking off the brass buttons. Elijah imagined him snatching it off a clothesline. Rainwater had collected in his hat brim, in his beard, the crevasses in his face and grooves between his knuckles. Cornbread passed him on his way out, and the two men gave each other a slight nod. Soon as he stepped off the wagon, Elijah noticed something different about Redbone. His gait had slowed, grown weaker.

Elijah ran to meet him. "Well, good evenin', son," said Redbone. "I guess I made it just in time." There was a Southern twang to his accent, and his voice squeaked like he needed oil on his vocal chords. He smelled different; wrinkling his nose, Elijah realized Redbone had buried his natural odor under some pungent grease. All of the man's whispered majesty was gone, replaced with a mask of wretchedness. Digging a hand into the boy's shoulder, Redbone leaned on it, walking with Elijah all the way to the door. Elijah hated being used as a cane, especially since he knew his mentor could walk. But Mr. Redbone kept on acting old. He seemed to take a century to do everything, and Elijah's older brothers were pulling out chairs for him, taking his new coat for him.

Elijah sat down, looked around the table. Pa, David, Joe and Tom on one side; himself, Mister Redbone and Mama on the other. The sight of them all together made his head feel woozy. "Mister Redbone…" Pa began.

"Please, call me Josiah. Do you mind if I say grace?"

Pa waved a hand. "By all means." Feeling relieved, Elijah settled in. He didn't expect Redbone to tell the truth about their job, but he expected a good yarn about traveling around Europe or the Caribbean jungles. Redbone had to have all sorts of stories.

"Thank you," Mr. Redbone said creakily, steepling his slender fingers together. He made a deep murmuring in his throat. "Lord God..." After saying the prayer, Mr. Redbone started eating. Elijah watched him scoop up mashed potatoes with a fork, bring them slowly to his puckered lips and slurp them down.

Finally, Pa said, "Where you from, Josiah?"

"Hunh?" Mr. Redbone blinked at him a few times. "Why, I'm from Mississippi. Jackson, 's matter o' fact. You know the Pearsons?"

"Can't say I do."

"Old white family. My family lived on their plantation after the emancipation." On that note, he went on for almost fifteen minutes about the details of planting corn. "Well, I watched my daddy rack up so much debt, I just ran off. Lived as a dockworker in New Orleans. That lasted 'til I caught the dysentery. I was a Pullman porter for a coupla years. Went to Chicago, got into some trouble 'long the way. Nice town, Chicago." He stopped talking to count the number of peas on his plate. "Where was I? Ah, yes, Chicago. Round 'bout, well, I guess it was twenty years back, I got a job sellin' shoes. This company's got offices all over the country. Thing is, they got us negroes to go down to negro towns like this one. So's I travel all year. I like Bogota. Lots of trees. Funny thing 'bout trees is…"

Mr. Redbone proceeded to talk about Mississippi trees, in great detail. Elijah stifled a yawn. Tom started nodding off. His two older brothers excused themselves to go wash everyone's plates.

Pa put his elbows on the table. "We love Elijah," he said, fixing the old man with a stare. "We love him, but the boy's always been a bit touched. Runnin' off, seein' things that ain't there."

*They* are *there,* Elijah wanted to say, but he knew Mr. Redbone wouldn't approve.

Redbone tapped the plate with his fork. "I know all about touched kids," he said. "And I know Elijah ain't one of 'em. When I lived in Chicago, all them touched kids would be round my apartment, drinkin' whiskey and smokin'. One o' the little demons even broke my window. Can you imagine that?"

"What I mean," said Pa, "is that Elijah don't always think straight…"

"Touched kids!" Redbone threw up his arms. "Where are their parents, I ask you?"

When Mr. Redbone got up to leave, Elijah once again served as his cane. The old man stopped by the doorway to bend down, slowly, achingly, and touch the top of Simon's head as the baby played with his pickanniny doll. "Where'd my hat get to?" Redbone asked, looking around.

"It on your head," Elijah droned. Reaching up, Redbone touched the brim, smiled in surprise. Nobody had talked about whether Elijah could keep his job, so he ran to Pa, tugging on his hand.

"Can I still be his assistant?" Elijah asked. "Please? Can I?"

"Yeah, yeah," said Pa, eating the last bits of chicken. "Lord know that man could use some company. Just be back before dinnertime."

"Elijah!" said Mama. "Can't you see he need help gettin' in his wagon?"

With a grin, Elijah ran outside, to where Mr. Redbone feebly tried to put his foot on the step. "Why was you fakin' in there?" he asked, climbing on the seat and offering his hand.

"I wasn't," said Mr. Redbone in his deep voice, stepping easily onto the seat.

"None o' that happened to you. You wasn't no porter."

"But it happened to somebody," said Mr. Redbone, "so it was true. I merely borrowed it." Sometimes Elijah thought Redbone was preparing him for a life as a flim-flam artist, and didn't care if Redbone knew he was thinking it.

"They're called social lies, Elijah," Mr. Redbone said with a sigh. "You tell them to make people feel comfortable. Your parents feel comfortable thinking I'm an old sharecropper who fell on hard times. A professional knows when to hide certain things, and you want to be a professional."

"That's right," said Elijah. "But…It still ain't right to talk 'bout somebody else life like it's your'n."

"In the end, there's only one story," said the old man. "Everybody's little story is a part of it, but it's one story. Give your mother my thanks for the meal. And take these." He handed Elijah six pairs of shoes, one for each of the family members who could walk. "As a gift. Now off with you." Elijah carried the armful of shoes back to the cabin. With excited looks, his brothers ran to meet him. Giving Elijah a nod, Mr. Redbone buttoned all five buttons on his coat, right up to the collar.

## Chapter Five
## King of the Castle

Four weeks after they found Maggie, Elijah came running to Mr. Redbone's cabin, fast enough to outrace the waking sun over the hill's crest. He felt this would be the day, and, sure enough, Redbone stood outside in his coat and hat, almost stately in his tattered threads. "You're going to stick close to me this time," he said. "Get Denny ready."

Elijah nearly jumped for joy. He hitched Denny to the wagon, feeding her carrots. "How we gon' find 'em?" Elijah asked.

"I have some clues as to where they are," said Mr. Redbone. "Rumors, whispers. We will follow the train tracks."

Elijah remembered the boredom of their last trip. "Can we go fast this time?"

"Fast, you say?" Mr. Redbone smiled, climbing on the wagon. "Denny here could give it a try. Giddyup, ha!" Mr. Redbone flicked the reins hard. Denny slowly turned her head, doing what Elijah could only guess was the donkey version of rolling her eyes.

For a while they clip-clopped alongside the tracks. Mr. Redbone pulled tobacco from a tin, rolled and lit a cigarette. "Me and Jimmy pick up things 'round here," Elijah said. "Shiny rocks and clothes and stuff. And the white folk come by in trains and throw us money, but sometime they laugh at us."

"Laugh at them," said Mr. Redbone. "They pay for the same things you just find by the tracks." A train roared by, but the men sitting in the open car doors weren't white passengers or laborers on their way to the quarry. Chained together, they were black men in black- and white-striped uniforms, their faces a sullen gray. Tobacco-chomping white men stood over them, cradling rifles. Mr. Redbone tipped his hat in salute to the black men.

Through the branches, Elijah saw a cabin built on stilts over marsh water. Rain had swollen the water so it touched the dangling leaves of the willows. Reeds grew jungle-like under the cabin, while atop the porch an old negro woman hung her clothes over the railing. Wearing many skirts and bare-chested, her breasts hanging to her navel. Elijah knew from Pa that hoodoo people lived in those cabins, and they generally didn't mingle with God-fearing negroes. He'd been told to stay away, but now he wondered if he could talk to them someday about the things they knew. As soon as he thought it, he noticed Redbone's smile.

Around midday, Mr. Redbone stopped the wagon and ventured into the trees. Looking close, Elijah saw a tent that looked more like a cave, and a man inside who looked like a huddled bear. A cloth bundle hung from a tree branch overhead. Mr. Redbone stooped low, handed the man a Mercury dime.

"Did you hear anything about the escape?" Mr. Redbone asked.

"Oh, yes." The man had a voice like steel scraping stone. "One of their little birds flew the coop. But I hear they clipped his wings not far yonder. I could tell you where, for a little extra help."

"That is perfectly alright for today." Elijah had no idea what they were talking about. Standing up, the tall ragged vagabond thanked the squat squalid vagabond for his time. The hobo shouted curses after him.

"You'll be glad to know we're on the right track," Mr. Redbone informed Elijah.

"Who that man?" asked Elijah.

"Just one of our ears," said Mr. Redbone. "He hears things."

"But he ain't say much," said Elijah, before remembering Redbone's talents.

"He'd tell me for another dime," Mr. Redbone replied, "but he'd already said enough. I know exactly where the child is."

"You shoulda paid 'im more," said Elijah, and Mr. Redbone just lashed the donkey. As the wagon started to move again, Elijah grabbed a dime off the footrest and tossed it to the hobo. He grinned up at Redbone, who simply grumbled.

Time passed. The amber sunlight trembled along the treetops. "I'll tell you a story," said Mr. Redbone. "Long ago, in the days when your father's father could only crawl, there was a doctor who had three sons. He lived in New York City, and was a man of great dignity. He had a great mustache, and a great big belly, to let everyone know he enjoyed fine meals. One day he did not come home, and his family believed him dead. His youngest son was a dandy who loved to play at cards. For weeks he asked, 'Hey, where's fathuh? It's been too long!' And his brothers said, 'Whassamatta? He's obviously dead. Why don't'cha help us take care o' Ma, instead'a wastin' time?' But the youngest questioned, and he complained, and he begged and needled until finally they said, 'He went to Brooklyn. Let's go to Brooklyn just to shut you up.' And wouldn't you know they found their father in Brooklyn? He was dead. Most assuredly dead. A pile of bones. Well, the youngest put the bones together. Then the middle son put skin on him. Then the eldest, who was a doctor himself, brought their father back to life, as physicians are wont to do. The young men cried and hugged their father and held a party in celebration. The good doctor called a toast, and said, 'Though I love all three of you, only one of you gets my beloved pocket watch as a sign of gratitude.' All three said, 'Me, me, me,' acting quite like children. In the end, he gave his watch to the youngest, and his son's son owns it to this day. Now, what do you think the meaning of the story is?"

Elijah could hear a trolley car screech, and the din of many voices, and the clink of glasses. "That the youngest deserved it," he said, "because he was the one who asked about the father."

"The meaning," said Mr. Redbone, "is never trust a gambler! He always has an ace up his sleeve. This particular ace earned him the watch."

"I like Cornbread's stories better." Cornbread told him about seeing a mountain for the first time, and how it was the biggest thing in the world besides sky. Cornbread told him that snow was like little scraps of paper that melted on the skin. "Cornbread's got all kinda stories. I think he's just as smart as you are."

"You truly love your cousin," Redbone said with an approving tone, leading them down a path that curved away from the track. "He is fortunate to have you."

It seemed, of all things large and small, the idea of family appealed most to the traveling salesman. Elijah wondered if he had family, a real one, and he envisioned Redbone's brothers springing up from the ground like seeds all planted together.

The forest receded into open grassland, and they followed a dirt road lined with telegraph poles. Elijah gawked at the landscape, thinking for a moment they'd left Mississippi altogether. *You're being stupid,* he thought, but this place still felt new and exciting. Closing his eyes, he thought of the third candle. An image popped in his head so fast it startled him. It wavered, but he held fast to it like he would a wriggling fish, concentrating until it grew clear as day: a brown blur leaping among the rocks with grace that a mountain goat would envy.

"He climbin' over them rocks over there." Elijah pointed to a nearby ridge of low foothills. "You think it'll be hard to get 'im?"

"Try following a child through the Brazilian rainforest for five days," said Mr. Redbone, "or the Arab desert for a week or two. Let's go."

"I'ma go by myself!" Mr. Redbone didn't think he could do it, not after Maggie. Before the old man could object, Elijah took off toward the hills. Scrambling up the boulder-strewn slope, he slipped and cut his palm on a stone. Wincing in pain, he sucked on the cut and continued, following the salty scent of brine to a ravine filled with garbage. A long-legged boy crouched behind a wall of trash, peering nervously at Elijah.

"Don't worry," said Elijah. "I'm comin' to take you home."

"I don't wanna go," said the curly-haired boy, who wore knee-length pants and a blue- and white-striped shirt.

"What your name?" Elijah asked, real patient, like Mr. Redbone told him to. Whoever this kid was, he probably wasn't used to people being considerate, so Elijah would be extra nice.

"Andy," said the boy. "Just let me alone."

This wasn't going too well. "You lost," said Elijah, "and you know you lost. C'mon, it'll be okay. I'm tryin'a *help* you."

"I ain't gotta do what you say!" Andy sprang up, ready to flee. Sighing, Elijah threw a rock at the garbage, knocking rotten fruit in Andy's face. Andy looked dumbfounded. Elijah put his hands on his hips and laughed.

"Ha! I bet you can't stop me from knockin' down that whole wall."

"Yeah I can!" Andy spat.

"Then defend your castle!" Laughing, Elijah flung everything he could find at Andy's garbage wall. Stones, chair legs, a beat-up trumpet, a tattered book of Charlie Chaplin paper dolls. Andy fired back, splattering Elijah with a rotten banana. Elijah ducked behind his own trash castle. Back and forth, they hurled buckets, newspapers, rusty nails, spade shovels, doll babies.

"Archers to the front! Ready! Aim! Fire!" Elijah threw a cracked fishing pole, knocked off a chuck of Andy's castle.

"Cannonball!" Andy crowed, hurling a deflated ball that almost took Elijah's head off. A barrage of soup cans riddled his battlements. Elijah looked like a swamp creature, coated in mud and food. He smelled like a wet animal. *Jimmy would love this,* he thought, panting and laughing at the same time. Andy didn't even seem winded, not a scratch or stain on his body.

"Creymark!" Elijah charged Andy's trash castle. Grimacing, the other boy retreated. Elijah howled in triumph, his stretched-out shadow lapping at the shadowless boy's heels. Smelling Mr. Redbone, he turned to see the man sitting atop the ravine, a serene smile on his face. God only knew how long he'd been watching them. For a few minutes, Elijah had forgotten the old man, or even that Andy wasn't a normal boy.

He scrambled on top of his trash castle. "Welcome, my lord," he called, bowing, "to the domain of King Creymark! Do you wish to attack Castle Creymark? I'ma strike you down!" He shook a stick in challenge.

"No, I'ma be king o' the castle!" Andy declared to Mr. Redbone, running to his fort. Elijah slipped off the trash heap, fell in a puddle. Sprawled out, he laughed until he wheezed.

Suddenly, something large hurtled through the air, demolishing Elijah's castle and landing in a heap not far from him. Dressed in a black- and white-striped uniform, a broken chain clamped around its ankle, limbs twisted in impossible positions. In place of a head it had a stump crawling with engorged maggots. Elijah scrunched his nose at the unmistakable reek of human shit. Horrified, he scurried away from it on hands and knees.

Andy skipped past him, right into Mr. Redbone's arms. "Ha ha ha," he sang, "I'm king o' the castle!"

Two days after he found Andy, Elijah was running to Berger's Hill from his cabin, when he saw Jimmy sitting by the road. The other boy waved casually, like they'd ran into each other by chance.

"Hey, 'Lijah," he said. "You goin'a work?"

"Yep. I can't talk right now…"

"You always workin'. When're we gon' go fishin'?"

"I don't know. Just go play by yourself." Even as he said the words, he felt guilty. With his trembling mouth, Jimmy reminded him of one of the lost children. Somehow, he had time for them, but not his best friend. "Alright. Let's fish after work. I'll be at the creek before sundown."

"Okay!" Jimmy gave a big gap-toothed grin. They walked with each other halfway to Berger's Hill, raced the other half. Jimmy parted from him at the bottom and padded back the way they came on his bare feet.

Elijah and Mr. Redbone sat outside the hut, patching up shoes with gum. Mr. Redbone poured Elijah a bowl of onion stew. His mouth watering, Elijah breathed in the spicy steam, tenderly chewed the hot morsels. Afterward, he lay on his belly in the grass, the food warm inside him.

"Elijah," said Mr. Redbone, "about what you saw last time…"

"I don't care," Elijah said, almost offended. "I done seen Manboy's body, too. It ain't no big deal. I'm just mad that boy think he king o' the castle." Andy had made fun of Elijah on the trip back, too. "I ain't the kinda person who get upset 'bout everythin'. My brother Tom cry all the time. He cry even when he stub his toe. Now, I'm like Pa. He only cried once, when Tom was born. Prob'ly 'cause it wasn't long after Uncle Cornelius died." Elijah had never made the connection in all the years since that day. His first real memory: Mama sitting calm and upright amid blood-spattered bedsheets while Pa cried as loud as the wailing red newborn in the midwife's arms, and now Elijah understood why.

Twelve people died during the Bad Day. No negro in Bogota could have survived without their hope for the future shattered.

Mr. Redbone's contemplative gaze interrupted his thoughts. Elijah smiled at him, defiantly. "You can't say I did bad wit' Andy. I messed up wit' Maggie, but Andy was waitin' there for you. I kept 'im in them hills playin'. Admit it; that took skill."

Mr. Redbone chuckled. "It did," he said. "It most certainly did."

"I even know where you take the chillun!"

"And where is that?" Redbone asked, the look of amusement never leaving his face.

"Heaven," said Elijah. "Where ever'body go. Ever'body gots a soul, and when you die, your soul go to Heaven. I guess that make you some kinda angel or sum'n."

To his disappointment, Redbone neither confirmed nor denied. He simply pointed to the bottom of his shoe. "Elijah," he said, "*this* is the sole."

For the life of him, Elijah didn't know what he meant. No matter. Chewing a blade of grass, he absentmindedly clicked the heels of his shoes together, confident he'd figure it out.

"Here," said Mr. Redbone, "let me show you something." He extended his hand. "Be warned. This will take all your concentration. Close your eyes."

Taking his hand, Elijah did as he was told. Mr. Redbone's touch felt like warm milk. "You want to see where they go. Concentrate on me." Elijah let Mr. Redbone's smell fill his body until he felt light as air. Redbone's thoughts wriggled like worms into his conscious. When Elijah opened his eyes, he stood in a wood like Bogota, only somehow more familiar, and hotter. Hot enough to squeeze every drop of water out his body. "Yes! You see it!" Mr. Redbone's hand anchored him fast in that world. Palm leaves blazed orange and purple and red. He heard unfamiliar animal sounds: a cackle from the trees, a low growl from the brush. Through the vine curtains, he saw a great fire. Huts stood behind it, hazy in the shimmering waves of heat. The fire grew brighter, hotter, so hot the world went white…

He opened his eyes, found himself again on Berger's Hill, hand held up but holding nothing. A smiling Mr. Redbone stood several yards behind him. "When I let go o' your hand?" Elijah asked. The familiar world rushed back to him, dull and colorless.

"Almost right after you took it," Mr. Redbone said proudly. "I think, if you really wanted to see where they go, all you have to do is look. Specialist."

*Specialist*. Sighing, Elijah lay on his back and closed his eyes. The vision left him lightheaded. Everything he felt in that strange wood baffled him. All he knew for certain was he felt *something*, and did it on his own.

## Chapter Six
## The Lost Boy

Elijah skipped over the Watchaloo Creek bridge, proud of his accomplishment that day. He wanted to follow Mr. Redbone everywhere, finding children, leading them home. Jimmy was nowhere in sight, and Elijah shrugged it off. To his surprise, Cornbread met him between the bridge and the cabin. Elijah ran to his cousin, finger-pistol blazing. "Pow pow pow!"

Cornbread picked up Elijah, swung him around. He smiled, but Elijah saw the sadness in his eyes, and knew his heart was heavy as stone. "What happen, Cornbread?"

"Nothin', o' course." Behind Cornbread's smile the wells had dried up. Behind Cornbread's smile the sun would never rise. "Why would you ask that?"

Elijah shrugged. "Ain't it dinnertime? Let's go eat."

Cornbread sat on a rock. "Naw, dinner ain't ready. 'Sides, you know your mama would just have you cookin'. Maybe if we don't go just yet, she won't miss us." Elijah remembered when Manboy died. All the grownups had the same everything-alright attitude Cornbread had now. But Cornbread wouldn't hide anything from him.

"C'mon, you wanna learn guitar? I'll teach you." Cornbread didn't wait for an answer. He cuffed Elijah's cheek playfully. "You lookin' a little F.F.F. right now, 'Lijah. Didn't you say you wanna learn? Here,

'Dixie' is an easy one for beginners. Watch my fingers, now." Cornbread strummed the familiar tune. "*Well I wish I was in the land of cotton, old times der am not forgotten, look away! Look away...*" While Cornbread played, Elijah started walking.

"I'ma go home," he said. Cornbread grabbed his shoulder so hard he gasped.

"That ain't happenin'." Cornbread's voice turned deadly serious. Elijah pushed him off and ran for the cabin. " 'Lijah! Please! You can't go in there!" Elijah didn't want to look at Cornbread, the only person in the world he thought would never lie to him. Reaching the house, he saw Ma, Pa and three other grownups inside, standing around what looked like a red bedsheet over a lump of coals. He started to move forward, when he saw a small hand sticking out from under the sheet. A cold feeling started in his stomach, spreading until it filled his body. His legs turned to jelly. He barely felt Cornbread's hand on his shoulder, barely heard his cousin's whispered words.

"Strength, 'Lijah. Strength."

The grownups tried to comfort him, but he didn't see them, or hear them. Mama tried to feed him, but the food was ash in his mouth. Sitting on the stoop, words drifted to him from inside the cabin.

"...Murder..."

"...White men..."

"...Castrated..."

It seemed like every negro in town gathered at his house. Elijah felt hot, suffocated by the people milling about. Every face was slack with sorrow, or twisted in rage. The muffled words from the cabin turned to shouting.

"A child, Earl!" The enraged voice belonged to one of the sharecroppers who lived down the road. "They did it 'cause he wouldn't get out the way o' their car! That's what it takes for these animals to kill our children?"

"We can't let them get away with it," said another man. "Not this time."

"But what can we do?" Pa's voice. Not a question, but a reminder to all the men.

"We need to be rational." Cornbread. "Earl's right. What'll we do? Fight 'em?"

"Says the drunk whoremonger." The sharecropper. "They killed a child!"

"I'll forget you said that." Cornbread.

"Stop it! Both o' y'all!" Pa.

"He shouldn'a been playin' by the creek," Mama said, "but they ain't had to do 'im like that. Damned monsters. Damn."

Once in a while, a hand touched Elijah's shoulder, and he would shrug it off. None of them could understand how he felt. Guilt was a wild beast raging and tearing inside him. An image burned in his brain: a limp, broken body in the creek. Fish nibbling his friend's face, Jimmy's blood swirling downstream. He had seen the candle. For weeks, he saw it dim. As the day wore on Elijah became a shade, thin and sullen, alone with his guilt.

He only moved at one point. Tom took Simon outside, and the idiot was smiling. Settling the baby down, he got on all fours and took the little pickaninny doll out his back pocket. "Fee fi fo fum!" he said, walking the doll toward Simon, making the baby giggle. Elijah got up, grabbed the doll out his hand and threw it. It didn't go far, landing without noise in the woodpile. When Tom stood up, Elijah pushed him back down. Tom cried. Simon cried. Still just as miserable, Elijah sat back in his spot. Nobody bothered him, after that.

The sheriff showed up in his Model T. A white man in his mid-thirties, he walked through the crowd of negroes like he owned the place. Stopping, he took a look around at all those gathered, as if taking note. Elijah averted his eyes, noticing that many grownups did the same. "What's this I hear about this boy you found?" the sheriff asked Pa as he entered. "Hit his head on a rock or somethin'?"

Rage, dark and all-consuming, interrupted Elijah's sorrow. Everyone there knew who killed Jimmy, just as they knew there would be no justice. Some white men, upset that he blocked their car on the road. Elijah knew there would be no trial. If there was, Jimmy's killers would go free within a day and get a round of drinks from their friends at the bar. They'd probably be elected to town council. Villains, the whole bunch of them. Devils.

Five minutes later, the sheriff stepped outside, took a deep sigh. "Nothin' to see here, folks," he told the grownups. "I suggest y'all go home now." He looked down at Elijah. "How you holdin' up there, boy?"

"Go to Hell," Elijah told him. The white man stared at him in dumb shock, then walked to his automobile, revolver bouncing on his hip. Elijah felt only a small delight at his outburst. *Maybe now they'll kill me, too,* he thought matter-of-factly. *That's what they do.*

"Whatever happened," he heard Pa say, quieting down the other grumbling men, "we can't all be here. You saw the way he looked at us. We don't need them crackers gettin' suspicious."

Mr. Jessup arrived with one of his sons. They each carried a rifle, and demanded to speak to Pa. Holding his hands up and open, Pa met them on the lawn. The conversation was short, questions and answers. Yes, the boy was killed on his land. No, he didn't live there. His parents weren't renters. This seemed to satisfy the landlord, who looked over the women and children outside. His gaze was iron. "Wrap this up," was his order to Pa, and then he left, too.

A half-moon appeared in the sky, a silver scythe poised above Elijah. The awful truth repeated like a mantra in his head: *You saw the candle and you did nothing.*

An old man came to the cabin, leaning on Cornbread's arm, weak as straw. Jimmy's guardian, Elijah realized, watching him strap Jimmy's bedsheet-shrouded corpse to the back of a mule and begin the lonely trek back to the river. Gradually, the grownups drifted away like specters in the night, to lock their doors and warn their children of what happened to Jimmy Ketchum. Only the Creymarks remained. Elijah heard Pa say, "Go talk to 'im, Cornbread."

"Why?" Cornbread sounded bone-tired. "Just let 'im alone for a while."

"Let 'im alone? You was s'posed to keep 'im away. He wasn't s'posed to see it!"

"Why should we lie to the boy, Earl?" Cornbread shot back. "He woulda found out anyway."

"He wasn't s'posed to *see*. This one thing I ask of you, and you can't do it…Where you goin'? You gotta be jokin'. You jokin', right?"

"Naw," said Cornbread. "I don't need to listen'a this shit."

"After all that happened—after this!—you actually goin'? Have you lost your right mind?"

"Maybe I have. I'm gonna go to town, get my twenty dollars from Sam and split." Elijah heard Cornbread throw on his duster. "I always hated this fuckin' place."

"You gon' get your money?" Pa laughed with venom. "You actually think a white man would consider himself in your debt?" Even as he yelled, Cornbread kept walking.

"Cornelius!" Elijah had never heard Pa this mad. "Elijah needs you now! If you ever gave a damn 'bout this family, you gon' stay put!"

Cornbread stormed out the house, slamming the door behind him. He stopped by Elijah, but Elijah wouldn't look at him. Right now he hated Cornbread. Hated him as much as the white men who killed Jimmy, though he didn't know why. He wanted Cornbread to just go to his beer hall and play his stupid guitar and never come near the family again. Sighing, Cornbread headed down the path, his duster blowing behind him. Elijah watched him disappear from sight.

" 'Lijah!"

Elijah made the mistake of looking. In that instant he saw him, as alive as yesterday. Nothing had changed. Wearing dirty overalls, hair in tangled naps, kicking dust off the road. When their eyes met Jimmy grinned ear to ear, that look of playful excitement Elijah knew so well. " 'Lijah! C'mon, let's go play."

The sight of him pierced Elijah like a dagger. He fell to the ground, pulled his head under his arms. He didn't want to see. He wanted to shut out the world until he woke from this nightmare. *Why did I look? Why did I look?*

" 'Lijah! 'Lijah, what happen?"

"Get away from me!" He ran. Blinded by tears, he tripped over the washtub, fell hard on the grass.

"What I do, huh? What I do now?" Jimmy sounded hurt from

Elijah's rejection, but all Elijah heard in his voice was *You knew.*

"I ain't know'd it was gon' be you! I woulda done sum'n!"

"Why you makin' me run, 'Lijah? C'mon, you know you faster'n me." But Jimmy got closer every second, and Elijah ran from his suddenly living friend. Jimmy's icy fingertips brushed his shoulder, making him jump. Elijah backed against a tree, terrified by the realness of him. The gap in his front teeth, the smell of fish, the genuine sadness in his eyes.

"Please go away!" he whimpered, shutting his eyes. "Please!" Any moment, he expected Jimmy to grab him, freeze him to death. Gripped by fear, he slowly realized the clearing had gone quiet.

Opening his eyes, he saw Jimmy seated on a rock. Mister Redbone knelt in front of him, talking soothingly, his weathered face frowning in pity. Jimmy cast tearful glances at his friend. Elijah could see the wagon through the trees, Denny stomping her hooves impatiently.

"Just give him time," Mr. Redbone told him.

"I don't wanna go wit' you," Jimmy sniffed. "I wanna stay wit' 'Lijah."

"Your time to be with Elijah will come."

"No! No, no, no! I don't know you! Get away from me!" Jimmy's anger hit the clearing around the cabin like a cyclone. Horrified, Elijah watched the world go mad; small trees uprooted, shirts blew off the laundry line. Stones rose from the ground and flew at the cabin, battering it with rage unreasonable. All the while Jimmy ran in a circle, hugging himself, gritting his teeth and crying. Mr. Redbone walked right into the eye of the storm, grabbed Jimmy and slung him unceremoniously over his shoulder. Jimmy kicked and screamed all the way to the wagon. "Lemme go, damnit! Lemme go!"

Elijah wanted to tell Mr. Redbone to stay and somehow explain all this to him, but the words died in his throat. Mr. Redbone would leave him. Even Cornbread had gone away to be with the white people. Suddenly, Mr. Redbone gave him a sharp glare, which softened into a look as pitying as the one he gave Jimmy. "Go inside, Elijah." And he was gone.

" 'Lijah!" He heard Pa's voice. " 'Lijah! Where you at?" Elijah ran into the woods, the last candle flickering before his eyes.

## Chapter Seven
## The Last Candle

"You should not be here."

Elijah wearily acknowledged Mr. Redbone's arrival at the hut. Covered in dirt and scratches, he sat cross-legged in front of the last candle. For hours he'd concentrated on it, searching for a face, but none popped into his mind. At one point he fell asleep, but the candle invaded his dreams, its flame shrinking to a speck and extinguishing from existence. Even now, it flickered like a faint breeze could blow it out. The four others, once red, stood gray in the darkness. Jimmy's candle glared at him in condemnation.

"Who is it?" Elijah asked, his voice hoarse. He had cried his eyes dry. He tried to keep his mind blank, in case Mr. Redbone decided to steal his thoughts.

"You should go home," Mr. Redbone said darkly. "This is not the night to be running about. I assure you, your father and brothers are looking for you. If you had any regard for your family, you would have stayed put."

"Who is it?" Elijah repeated. Who would be taken from him next?

Sitting slumped at the table, Mr. Redbone never looked older than now. Thin and frail, he seemed to melt into his clothes. He poured a shot of whiskey and downed it in a heartbeat. "I made a mistake," he told the glass, pouring another shot. "Why'd it have to be a child?"

"You told me we could relight the candles," Elijah blurted, delirious with hope. "You said…"

"Silence!" Mr. Redbone's anger blasted Elijah with the heat of an inferno. The boy shrank against the floor in fright. "Shut your mouth and listen to me! I'm very sorry about what happened to your friend. More than you know. But nobody could have known. Even we, with all our talents, could not have known!" Mr. Redbone's inferno cooled. Hoisting Elijah by his shoulders, he placed him on the stool. "I'm sorry I got upset at you, but you need to realize he's gone."

"Can I at least talk to 'im?" Elijah's voice sounded high in his own ears, like a spoiled brat. "If you took 'im, you can bring 'im back. Or take me to see 'im."

"We are the guides," Mr. Redbone said in a tone that told Elijah he would tolerate no more argument. "What you talk of is foolishness, and I was a fool for coddling you with false hope."

Elijah felt faint. The room spun around him. White people kept killing and killing. Mr. Redbone could stop them, but he chose not to.

How could he be so cruel? "I assure you, Jimmy does not blame you for what happened," Redbone said.

"I hate you!" Elijah recoiled from his outstretched hand. Why couldn't he use his talents for good, like the Magic Man? Was it as simple as lighting a candle? They could have all lived. Manboy, Maggie, Andy, Jimmy. His uncle and everyone who died on the Bad Day. The men in Cornbread's platoon could have lived, and Cornbread wouldn't be so sad.

"Those thirty-five boys," Mr. Redbone answered his thought, "wandering around that battlefield." He closed his eyes, and his voice held the sadness of the world. "They kept asking, 'Where am I?' 'How do I get home?' 'Where's Mama?' What was I supposed to tell them? It's times like that I hate my job. Times like when I took your friend. Manboy, Maggie…They lived full lives. They had no problem going with me. Maggie was especially happy about it." He smiled warmly. "That's the wonderful thing about children: you're so curious."

"But why Jimmy?" Elijah pleaded. "Why not them white men that killed 'im? Why can't they die? How come it gotta be…" Jimmy's sad face flashed through his mind, opening the floodgates. Fragments; half-remembered moments of fishing, roughhousing, eating dinner at his cabin; joking conversations, the words of which escaped him. Desperately, he tried to form complete memories of Jimmy like gathering the shards of a shattered glass.

"It don't even matter," Elijah whispered. "Ever since we born, all we doin' is dyin'."

"I like to think that the moment we're born is when we start living," Mr. Redbone replied. "One so young should not know such pain. Not when there are trees to climb and lakes to swim. You have not had an easy life, but I would have your dreams be happy." A pair of rake-thin arms wrapped around him, rocked him back and forth. Mr. Redbone's heat became a fire in coldest winter. His scent enveloped Elijah like a blanket. Elijah snuggled against his chest, letting the old man comfort him. In that moment he envied Jimmy, envied the children who got to take the journey with him. "You're a wonderful assistant. So enthusiastic, so excited. But you're too young."

"I did real good, huh?" Elijah asked, sleepily.

"You were excellent," Mr. Redbone crooned.

"Then you ain't never gon' lie to me, right?" He opened his heavy eyes, glanced into Redbone's, hoping to see some glimmer of humanity. But they were black, cold. "You'd tell me the truth if you knew sum'n, right?"

Mr. Redbone let out a low, rumbling sigh. Elijah pushed away from him. "Elijah," said Mr. Redbone, "you have to understand…" A new image filled Elijah's mind. A stone on Cemetery Hill:

Michael Cornelius Creymark, Jr.
Born 1896
Died 1920

"I had a feeling it was Cornbread." Mr. Redbone approached, face shadowed by his hat brim. The specter of death. "I followed him. Believe me, I wanted to find him before he sought you ought. I wanted to spare you that, at least. He went to town to get the pay his boss was holding out on, so he could quit. Everybody in town is on edge; they think the blacks are planning something. When Cornbread confronted him, the man and two of his goons tried to kill him. Cornbread fought his way out, killed them all. You don't just kill three white men without comeuppance. Believe me, I meant to spare you." To Elijah's ears, even his words of kindness dripped with evil. "You should go home and stay home. Don't worry; I'll catch him."

*Catch him?* Elijah felt like his head would explode. He looked to the last candle, at Cornbread's life flickering away. Mr. Redbone sensed his intentions, but not fast enough. Yanking the candle off the table just as the old man reached for it, Elijah held it before him as if warding off the devil Redbone. He held his breath, afraid he'd blow out the flame. The room felt hotter than Hell, but cold sweat beaded Elijah's skin. With infuriating calm, Redbone glared down on him. "There is no time," the old man said in annoyance. "They are almost upon him, a whole hunting party— Where are you going?"

Elijah ran outside. Carefully placing the candle on the ground, he jumped up, grasped the hourglass lantern hanging off the roof. Elijah crashed down, and the lantern with him. It shattered. He panicked for a second, then saw the lantern's candle burning among the shards. Sucking in his breath through clenched teeth, he carefully inched the two candles together.

"Not a good idea." Mr. Redbone stood in the doorway, arms folded. The old man's voice stopped his arm. "Do you honestly think that will work? What do you know of the power you trifle with?" Elijah felt like nothing more than a child, and an ignorant one at that. Mr. Redbone was old, and powerful, and knew more about the world than he ever could. What did his desires matter next to this man's knowledge? How could he hope to defy someone like this?

"Come inside, Elijah," Redbone continued. "I know you want to help your cousin, and, believe me, I understand." Harsh words, but sympathetic, like a father scolding his wayward son. "You made a mistake, but I forgive you. Now come inside, and we'll talk like we always have, as teacher and apprentice."

Elijah faltered, let the arm holding the last candle drop. He wanted forgiveness. He wanted hugs and love and sleep free of nightmares. He took a step, then another, to join the old man. Mr. Redbone smiled now. "That's a good boy," he said.

Elijah shook his head, snapped to attention. Just like that, the spell was broken.

"You would not dare!" The voice battered Elijah with its fury. The anger of a god. For that split second, Mr. Redbone appeared as a gloom hovering in the doorway, with promises of pain if Elijah continued. Iron hands gripped the boy's throat. He felt fear; terrible, sickening, but not that much worse than what he felt every day of his life. Staring defiantly into the dark, right at his mentor, Elijah put the flames together.

He didn't know what he expected. An explosion, a storm; something more earth-shattering than the silence that followed. When he pulled the red candle away, a new flame burned. Majestic, it bathed him in golden light. Elijah let out a cry of pure joy, laughing through his tears. It didn't matter what happened to him. Cornbread was safe.

"I'm sorry," said a raspy voice. Mr. Redbone sat in the doorway, like a marionette whose strings had been cut. "I should not have used that power on you. I'm so sorry." He glanced inside. "You got your wish. Look."

Elijah did as Mister Redbone told. Pure horror filled him.

Three sputtering candles had taken the place of Cornbread's.

"You know how they work," said Mr. Redbone. "If they can't get the one they want, anybody will do. That is why we are merely the guides. Even I don't know what will happen when we interfere."

"I'm so—" He choked on the apology. Mr. Redbone looked at him from behind a curtain of silver hair, unfathomable sadness etched on his face. None of this made sense. Everything was supposed to turn out okay.

Using the doorway for support, Mr. Redbone climbed to his feet. "I have a long night ahead of me, son. Let us hope that in the future you make better choices." His voice grew faint as the moth's wings. "Let's hope I can, as well."

Without knowing why, Elijah handed him the candle. The broken-down man took it carefully, nodded in thanks, holding it close like a newborn. With a dignified gait, he carried the light into the cabin. Like a saint presenting his beacon to the Lord. Mr. Redbone looked back at him. "Well, do you want to go home?"

Elijah almost asked why Redbone would help him after what he'd done, but he knew why. This was what Mr. Redbone did. Elijah took his hand. Darkness poured over him slowly, falteringly, Mr. Redbone's magic withered and exhausted. For a moment Elijah only saw blackness. Then he found himself no longer on Berger's Hill, but in a corner of the woods. Three lights weaved through the trees. Candles.

"Elijah!" Pa yelled. He saw Pa, David and Joe holding lanterns. His brothers put their arms around him, ushering him quickly back home.

***

Cousin Cornbread left without telling anyone goodbye. It was best that way. He'd probably hopped a train to far away, and he'd be the better for it. Ghosts haunted the Bogota woods, bearing torches and rope. Elijah sat by Mama, listening to her song. He was nothing special that night. Not a fetish-man, not an assistant. Just a frightened child praying to live until morning.

Pa had gotten the word out to a farmer with a mule, who then spread the warning through the woods. Elijah guessed what was happening all around Bogota. Negroes were abandoning their homes, hiding among the trees while the whites rampaged. When the smoke cleared, some would move to Louisiana, or up north. Others would return to burnt cabins, attempt to rebuild their lives. Standing resolutely by the window, Pa kept his gun ready, searching the dark for invaders.

Elijah watched the little girl outside their cabin melt into the night. He shut his crying eyes, denying his talents before they hurt anyone else. Yet, with the unthinking curiosity of the young, he looked back to the window. Mr. Redbone's words came to him, a promise of future days: *All you have to do is look.* Elijah strode right up to the window. Pa watched him, shocked. Looking deep in the dark, Elijah saw the lost girl.

"Go to Berger's Hill!" he shouted. "The red grass hill!" Pa clamped a hand over his mouth, but the girl heard him. Using his second sight, Elijah watched her travel to the rounded hill, a man and two boys waiting for her.

"Damnit!" said Pa. "We can't stay here! Grab the food! And blankets! Only what we need!" Elijah felt hands pushing him out the door, into the woods, where the whole family huddled among the bushes. Pa muttered curses as he watched their cabin through overhanging branches.

Within his mind, Elijah still saw the girl with Mr. Redbone and the boys, ready for their journey. He held onto that sight. "Pa, sum'n wrong wit' 'Lijah!" said Tom. "He havin' a spell or sum'n."

"Damn touched child!" Pa said. "Just cover his mouth so he don't yell again!" Elijah heard him as if from a hundred yards away. Smiling, he watched Redbone and the children enter the foreign, familiar forest.

The girl held one of the boy's hands. Other children emerged, seeming to sprout from the ground. Two by two, hundreds of them ran and skipped and cartwheeled over the soft soil. A python curled around a branch, hissing in welcome. Monkeys cackled their greeting. The guide in the well-worn suit strode before the children. They gathered round him, holding his arms, asking a hundred questions. "It'll all be answered, sweethearts," he said. "Don't dally. We're almost there. Two by two. John, hold Sarah's hand. It's up ahead, Richie. Two by two."

They came to the clearing where the fire burned. A heat so powerful it seemed to blast from all around them. Drums pounded from the very earth. The children danced around the fire, chanting. Folding his arms, the guide watched them with the satisfied smile of a father watching his children play. Around and around and faster, they danced. The guide grew taller, wider, taking his true form. His head elongated, coming to a peak at the top; his skin turned jet-black and smooth as marble. A gold crown sat atop his long head; cowry shells rattled in the bracelets along his arms, the threads of his thatch skirt. Towering over the children, he sang a verse and they answered. Short, simple call and response, sung to the beat of their hearts. Elijah heard the words in his mind, in a voice too pure for language. He joined in, answering Mr. Redbone's calls with the other children:

I come from the land of fire and grass
*Two by two, we go to the flame*
I hold all that is old, all that will come
*Two by two, we go to the flame*
I give it to children, I give it to my young
*Two by two, we go to the flame*
I give it to child nursing at mother's breast
*Two by two, we go to the flame*
To the wayward, the wanderers, the ones blind to hope

*Two by two, we go to the flame*
To the lost I give the flame that will burn again
*Two by two, we go to the flame*
*Two by two, we go to the flame...*

Over and over, they chanted. The distance between their worlds disappeared and Elijah was there, at the fire. In all the long years of his life he would never forget the pure bliss. Try as he might, Elijah could not see into the flame: the doorway that swallowed the children, never to return. Stars glittered in the guide's timeless gaze. Worlds were birthed and died under his outstretched arms. He urged his wayward children to return home. Two by two they leapt in the fire, sending embers into the sky. Following his beautiful voice, dancing, dancing, returning to the flame.

**Elwin Cotman** was born in Pittsburgh, Pennsylvania in 1984. In 2005, he graduated from the University of Pittsburgh with a degree in Creative Writing. In his time, Elwin has been a Wal-Mart employee, bookseller, middle school teacher, youth counselor and ESL instructor, and has finally found a job that pays less than any of those: fantasy writer. He currently resides in Lafayette, Louisiana and blogs at lookmanoagent.blogspot.com. This is his first collection.

**Rachel Dorrett** is a native of Baltimore, Maryland. She received her BFA from Carnegie Mellon University in 2010. Rachel is an artist who makes fantasy-based work, primarily conceptual designs of invented worlds. Much of her work focuses upon creating complex visual compositions based on narratives similar to that of folktales, and combines invented characters and spaces together.

Made in the USA
Middletown, DE
12 June 2016